SEIZED THE HEART OF THE REAPER

A Standalone Novel

JATORIA C.

D1528998

WANT TO BE A PART OF GRAND PENZ PUBLICATIONS?

To submit your manuscript to Grand Penz Publications, please send the first three chapters and synopsis to info@grandpenz.com

SYNOPSIS:

Egypt Harris's life was good two years ago. She had just graduated from Alabama State University with a master's degree in social work and decided to go out to the club with her sisters to celebrate her achievement. While they were out partying, she was approached by a guy named Vance, but she turned him down and continued celebrating with her sisters.

The next day, she received a message request on Facebook from Vance, and despite her gut feeling about him, she accepted it. They began messaging and talking to each other every day. After a few weeks of messaging every day, they agreed to meet up and chill.

Over the next few months, Egypt and Vance continue to talk every day and hang with each other often. Egypt thought he was a cool person and he acted like he was all about her, so when he asked her to be his girlfriend, she accepted.

After becoming his girlfriend, Vance changed and became a monster. He constantly cheated, was manipulative, and abusive toward her. She was getting fed up with their relationship and was close to her breaking point. He did the unthinkable one night, and she was done trying to make their relationship work. She tried to break it off with him for good and move on with her life but he refused to let her go. Egypt feared him and afraid he would end up killing her or her sisters.

Her sister called in a favor and got security for Egypt. Falling in love with the security was the furthest thing from Egypt's mind, but as the saying goes, the best love is unexpected. Her protector is rich, handsome, and very mysterious. She is drawn to him immediately but tries to ignore her attraction. Things turn serious for her and her protector quickly, but is love enough for her to stay when she finds out his secret?

Chapter One

EGYPT

"Girl, did you see what your man posted on Facebook about you?" my coworker Vee asked me. " Chile no I'm so use to that man running to Facebook lying that I don't pay his ass no attention" I replied. " His ass is crazy. He claims you put him out for no reason just so you can cheat on him" she told me. I shook my head. " Honey if people believe him that's them, but I'm about to head to my office so I can get up out of here" I told Vee. " Girl me too, I will see you tomorrow boo" Vee replied. I smiled and Vee turned to walk towards her unit. It was a lot more I could have said about me and my boyfriend Vance argument, but I knew better. I had to learn the hard way not to vent about my relationship with people, especially these hoes I worked with.

Hoes loved running to me with gossip about my man, like they wouldn't sit on his dick the first chance they got. I almost lost my job about six months ago when I caught one of my coworkers in my boyfriend's Facebook messages. Hoe was in my face, telling me I deserved better, but was in his messages, trying to sneak some dick. Of course, his grimy ass was entertaining the girl.

When I confronted him about her, he admitted they had been messaging each other, but they had not had sex with one another. He swore he didn't know me and the girl worked together, like that was supposed to make the situation any better. When I confronted the bitch, she got slick at the mouth like I wouldn't pop her in her shit at work. Silly hoe was talking about I was trying to beef with her about a nigga who was fucking everybody, but I was mad about her smiling in my face, then going behind my back on some sneak shit. If only they knew the hell I went through with my boyfriend, their asses would think twice before entertaining him.

Every time we broke up and I stopped responding to his messages, he ran to Facebook, talking shit about me. I hated being publicly embarrassed and I liked to keep my personal life private. I already knew he was making statuses, saying I looked ugly without filters or telling everybody I was a hoe. Hell, he was probably calling me a witch again, telling people I did magic on him. It did not matter that none of the shit he posted about me was true. I just hated the attention it brought to me. A part of me wished I had a sneaky link or a side nigga because he did not know what it meant to be faithful.

I broke up with him four days ago and kicked him out of the house.

I'd come home from work and decided to watch a movie in the living room instead of laying in my bed to watch TV. I went and sat on my couch and looked for the remote, but I didn't see it, so I checked between the cushions. When I reached inside the couch, I felt a box, so I pulled it out. It was an unopened box of Magnum condoms, size large. I went down into his man cave and snapped. I asked his ass where the condoms came from because we did not use condoms. I should have asked his ass why he was purchasing condoms in a large size, anyway, knowing they couldn't fit him, but that would have started a fight and I just wanted him to get the fuck out.

He swore the condoms belonged to his homeboy, Chris, but I knew he was lying. Chris was always at my house, but Chris was also in love with his baby momma. Chris and his baby momma had been together for over ten years, so I knew they were fucking without using protection.

Chris's baby momma dogged the fuck out of him. They had three kids together, but when she got mad at him, she would leave him with the kids and disappear for days. He always forgave her, though, and let her come back home. I think it was payback for the way he treated her in the past, so I minded my business.

Vance hated Chris's baby momma and always called his homeboy a pussy for putting up with her shit. At least his homeboy was putting effort into their relationship. I was so used to Vance cheating and acting an ass on me, I honestly stopped caring a long time ago.

My iPhone started vibrating in my purse again, and I knew I would have to answer him soon before he took things too far. I was done counseling the girls today and would be getting off work soon, so I pulled out my phone and unlocked it to see what he had to say. I worked at a mental health facility for kids under the age of nineteen. The facility kept the kids separated by their sex and age. I counseled the teenage girls between the ages of twelve and nineteen. I loved my job, and I had a great relationship with the girls, who came to me to be counseled.

Majority of them did not have family visit them, and being locked up in a mental health facility was a lot like being locked up in a juvenile detention camp. There was a lot of jealousy and fighting among the kids here. Vance had called me multiple times and sent six messages. I opened the last message he sent to read it.

. . .

Fckboy: answer the phone before I come to your job and shoot your car up

Fckboy: you stupid bitch don't nobody want you but me

Fckboy: bby please respond I'm sorry I'ma do better

Fckboy: I knw you see me calling nd texting you not gne respond

Fckboy: answer before I put all yo hoe ass sisters business on Facebook. Fuck all y'all!

Inhaling and exhaling, I finished reading the messages he'd sent to my phone and laid my head on my desk. I did not have any friends I associated with heavy. I didn't need any because I had two sisters who I did everything with. I knew if I did not respond soon, he would really start making statuses, talking about my sisters. I swear niggas were messier than bitches.

If his psycho ass would stop sneaking my phone and going through my group chat messages, he wouldn't know shit about them.

The last time we got into it and broke up, he posted statuses, talking shit about me all that day. When he saw I wasn't entertaining him like I normally did, he made a status about one of my sisters. He posted, saying how I wasn't a loyal friend and how my hoe ass friend stayed in my ear about my relationship but was running around, burning niggas. He didn't say my sister's name, but both of them knew who he was talking about. They were mad as fuck at me for a week because they thought I told him their business. I would never do anything like that. The sad part was, everybody from our city laughed and cheered him on when he started talking stupid on Facebook instead of telling his thirty-two-year-old ass to grow the fuck up.

He was the only grown man I knew who ran to Facebook about every little thing. He put on an image like he was so real and would call out anybody he felt had done him wrong, when, in reality, he lacked accountability and liked to bully me into forgiving him every time he fucked up.

I didn't understand why he treated me the way he did. Me and Vance had been in a relationship for two years and I had never cheated on him. I made my own money and I was patient while he tried to save enough money to get on his feet. I cooked, cleaned, and fucked him good. I really did not deserve the bullshit he put me through, and I was getting fed up with our whole relationship.

Me: Delete the statuses and promise me you will not post anything else. I am getting so tired of you fucking up and then showing out because you fucked up!

Fckboy: okay bby chill I'm about to delete all of em now. I'm leaving the hood soon and heading home. You gon cook?

Me: Yea Vance

Vance

This stupid ass bitch had finally responded to a nigga's messages. I'd been texting and calling her ever since she put me out four days ago. I had to threaten her to get her to respond.

I had been laid up at my aunt, Keisha's, house every night since Egypt kicked me out.

Egypt and I stayed fussing about these bitches I fucked, but I knew she would let me come back home, so I wasn't tripping.

She didn't know it, but every time she kicked me out, I still went and chilled at the house every day. I had an extra key made one day while she was taking a nap so I could always have a way in the crib when she took my key from me.

I got up and walked to Keisha's bedroom. Keisha stayed in a two-bedroom apartment in the hood, but she kept her apartment clean and food in her kitchen. Keisha had grown up in the hood, so she was cool with everybody and did not mind me stashing my shit there. I could leave my work with Keisha and send the fiends to her crib to pick up what they needed while I was at home with Egypt. She knew how serious I was about weighing my shit, so she made sure she bagged the right amount every time.

The door was open, and Keisha was laying on her bed, scrolling through her phone. She had on one of those red and white, one piece short sets with her ass hanging out the bottom.

I closed her room door and took off my shirt and slides.

"You gon' suck this big motherfucker?" I asked Keisha and got in bed with her. Keisha's freaky ass did not waste any time pulling my gym shorts and boxers down. She slowly sucked the head of my dick. I pushed her head all the way down and held it there. I hoped she choked.

Thirty seconds later, I let her head go and repeated the same shit until I felt like letting her head up. Keisha had spit rolling down her chin and one of her eyelashes was hanging from her tears.

"Toot that ass up," I told her, and slapped her on the ass.

Keisha stood up and took her clothes off. She had a big, cornbread fed ass. She was light skin with no titties, but her ass was fat enough, she didn't need them. She was about five feet and six inches tall and eight years older than me but looked good for her age.

After Keisha got naked, she climbed back on her bed and

tooted her ass up with an arch in her back. I got behind her and slammed my seven-inch dick in her pussy hard. I licked my thumb and stuck it up her ass. I fucked Keisha hard while using my thumb to stretch her ass out. She moaned and yelled.

Keisha had some fire ass head, but the pussy was worn out. Her shit was like an ocean. It got wet as fuck, but had no walls to grip my dick.

"You my bitch?" I asked and wrapped my hands around her weave. I slipped out her pussy and put my dick in her ass. Unlike her loose ass pussy, her ass stayed tight. I fucked her ass slowly and Keisha nutted, screaming and shaking. I felt my nut rising, but I tried to last a few more minutes.

A minute later, I pulled out and nutted on her ass. I slapped Keisha on the ass one more time to watch it jiggle and rubbed my nut all over her ass cheeks. I got off the bed and headed toward the shower. I could not risk waiting until I got home to take a shower because I didn't want Egypt to smell sex on me.

Keisha tried to get up and follow me to her bathroom, but I slammed the door in her face and locked it. She knew I wasn't about to let her shower with me. She stayed trying to be on some lovey-dovey type shit with me, but all I had for my hoes was hard dick. " Vance let me in" Keisha said knocking on her bathroom door. " Man chill out" I yelled back and cut on the shower.

Egypt had been tripping a lot lately about every little thing, so after I showered and put my clothes back on, I told Keisha I was dipping and headed to my car. I pulled off and drove toward the house.

Egypt and I stayed about twenty minutes away from the hood in a quiet neighborhood. The house was in a cul-de-sac, so there were only two other houses around us. Our house was a brick house with a big backyard. It was supposed to be a three-bedroom, two bathroom, but she had turned one of the rooms into my man cave so I could chill with my friends without her being up under us.

When I walked in the house, Egypt was at the stove, cooking. She could throw down in the kitchen, and whatever she was cooking smelled good as fuck.

"Hey, baby," I said and walked up behind her to hold her. Egypt was short, so I had to lean all the way down to wrap my arms around her. She didn't say anything back, so I knew she was still pissed about the condoms she'd found.

I was drunk as fuck one night when I bought them, and they fell out my pocket. I didn't realize I had lost them until the next day, but I never found them, so I let the shit go and bought a new pack. Egypt and Keisha were the only two bitches I fucked raw; everybody else, I wrapped up with, so I had to keep condoms on deck.

After a few minutes of holding Egypt, I let her go. I grabbed a beer out the fridge and went into my man cave to find a movie to watch. I found a movie on Tubi and relaxed in my recliner until the food was ready.

Egypt had cooked smothered pork chops, white rice, green beans, and corn bread. She fixed my plate and brought it to me, but she still wasn't speaking to me. After I finished eating, I put my plate in the sink. I didn't even bother going upstairs to climb in the bed with Egypt. I grabbed a blanket out the hall closet and relaxed in the recliner until I fell asleep.

Egypt

A week had passed since Vance had brought his ass back home and I hadn't had more than a few words to say to him. He'd mostly been in his man cave, and I'd been pulling extra shifts at work to avoid being around him. He had not tried to touch me, and I was grateful because I did not feel like putting on a performance.

Laying down in the bed beside him, I wondered how I'd let my life gets so far out of control. Life was good to me two years ago, before I met him.

I had just graduated from Alabama State University with a master's degree in social work. I'd worked hard for my degree and had maintained a 3.5 GPA all six years of college while working at night as a bartender.

After graduation, me and my two sisters, Jordan and Syria, decided to hit the strip club after we went out to eat. They had made reservations at Evangeline's as a graduation gift to me. Evangeline's was one of the most expensive restaurants in Tuscaloosa, and reservations had to be made months in advance. They had a lot of good food choices on their menu, but since we had decided to go out to the strip club afterward, I only ate a steak salad so I wouldn't be too full.

I was twenty-four years old and the middle sister. Jordan was the oldest sister at twenty-eight and Syria was the baby sister at twenty-three. We all favored each other, but both of my sisters were taller than me. I was only five feet tall with shoes on. I had pecan brown skin that was blemish free and a round ass face. My eyes were brown and small and I had a cute button nose. My favorite feature on my face was my lips. I had big, juicy ass lips and I loved it. My natural hair was thick as fuck and reached past my shoulders. I kept my hair in braids, though, because a bitch couldn't deal with doing hair every day. I knew I was pretty as fuck and was very confident.

Growing up, I was always told I looked like Gabrielle Union. I neither agreed nor disagreed. The only similarities I noticed was our skin color and smile. My breasts and ass were bigger than hers, but not by a whole lot.

After dinner, we headed to the liquor store and then we went to our older sister Jordan's house to get dressed. We started drinking and getting ready for the club. I knew we would not make it there before twelve because it took us forever to get ready. After my shower, I moisturized with body oil that had shea and cocoa butter in it. I put on a black Chanel bodycon dress with red heels and a matching red Chanel mini bag. I did not wear expensive perfume like everybody else I knew. I had a vanilla perfume that came from overseas that smelled great on me. It was the only perfume I wore, and it blended well with my body oil.

We did our makeup and headed out the door. The strip club was packed, and the line was long. We got in the skip line, though, and paid extra to walk right in.

"This shit lit! Let's go get us a drink!" Jordan yelled as soon as we got inside the strip club.

We headed to the bar, and I ordered a cup of Crown and a Bud Light. The club was packed, full of hood niggas, but I had grown up in the hood, so I was not impressed.

We paid to get a section and let loose, dancing and making Snapchat videos of us popping and shaking our asses all night.

After I finished my beer and got two more cups of Crown, I had to use the bathroom. I grabbed my empty beer bottle off the table and let my sisters know I would be right back. On the way back from the bathroom, I felt somebody bump me. I turned around, ready to bust a bitch in the head with my beer bottle, but instead, it was a nigga I had never met before, laughing like the shit was funny. He was dark skinned, stood about five feet eleven inches, had dreads that were in a Rasta head cap, and a mouth full of gold. He had on a blue Givenchy shirt, a pair of black Givenchy pants, and blue Nike Air Maxes. His outfit was fire as fuck, but I noticed he didn't have any jewelry on, and he didn't have any ones in his hand, either.

"What's good, ma?" he said after he stopped laughing. I turned to walk away, but he reached out and grabbed my hand. "Ay, let me get ya number?" he asked.

"No, thank you," I responded, and he nodded and let my hand go.

I felt a pain in my stomach while he was talking, but I thought I had butterflies, so I ignored it. I walked back to our section and told my sisters I wanted to get a chicken plate and head home.

The next night, I was laying in my bed, scrolling on Facebook, about three in the morning, and a notification popped up that I had gotten a message request. The message request was from the guy who had stopped me the night before in the club. He sent a message and told me to go to bed because only monsters stayed up at night. I responded, and he started messaging me every day. I had been single for over a year and was bored and lonely.

He told me he had gotten into trouble at a young age and made a mistake. He ended up doing time and had only been home a few months. He said he was single because every female he talked to had switched up on him when he was down and he wanted to focus on getting back on his feet.

After messaging each other for a few weeks, we started chilling and hanging out. He was cool as fuck and acted like he was all about me. After a couple months of talking, he asked me to be his girlfriend and I agreed. He moved in with me and my life had been hell ever since.

Vance

It had been over a week and Egypt was still acting funny. Every time she got mad, she wouldn't let me touch her and I wanted us to have sex. I left the hood early and headed home. When I made it there, I walked through the door and instantly got pissed. I was hungry and I didn't smell any food cooking. Egypt hasn't cooked since that first night I came back home. " Egypt" I yelled her name out but she didn't respond. I walked into our bedroom and she was laying on the bed watching tv. " Ay you didn't hear me calling your name" I asked Egypt? She didn't respond. " Now if I slap the fuck out of you for being a childish imma be wrong and why the fuck you ain't cooked?" I asked Egypt with an attitude. " Vance leave me alone. It's plenty of food in there and you know how to cook" she replied rolling her eyes. " Baby those condoms was not mine" I pleaded with her but she just turned her head and continued watching tv. I walked away before I lost my temper. I been sleeping in my man cave all week and this shit was getting tiring. I went to the kitchen to fix me something to eat and head downstairs into my man cave to relax. The next morning I woke up and went to check upstairs to see if Egypt had already left for work.

I needed to get back on her good side, so I texted her and told her I was laying in the bed, sick. I told her I was having bad stomach pains and had been throwing up all morning.

I hit my right-hand man, Chris, up and told him to close the trap down for the day. I did not trust those motherfuckers to do right without me being on the block to watch them. I would kill one of them niggas if some shit popped off with my dope or money.

I rolled a blunt and headed to the kitchen to cook. I decided to cook some chicken and rice for my girl to eat when she got off work. I took what I needed to make the food out and began cooking. Once the chicken was ready, I added the rice to let it finish cooking. I headed down to my man cave and counted my money while I waited on the food to cook.

When I met Egypt, I had only been home from prison a few months. Once we started kicking shit heavy, she let me move in with her so I could get on my feet. I told her I was trying to hustle to save up enough money to go legit and leave the streets alone, but I was lying. I never planned on leaving the hood. I was born in the hood, and I would die in the hood.

I had been saving money for two years while Egypt worked and paid all the bills. Money was the least of my concern, but Egypt didn't know that. I had almost six figures saved up and business was booming.

When I got out of prison, I only had a couple thousand dollars to my name and no car. When me and Egypt first started kicking it, I used to pull up on her in Chris's car. When I moved in with Egypt, she let me ride her car while she was at work or home. It took me a few months of hustling before I had enough bread to get my own car.

Egypt was different from the other bitches I fucked with. Yeah, those hoes would let me stash my dope and they fucked and sucked me, but Egypt helped me get on my shit.

I got up and walked back in the kitchen to fix my girl a plate. After I fixed her a plate, I grabbed my phone and went to a video I'd made a couple of weeks ago with this little thot from around the way. I pulled my dick out, spat in my hand, and started jacking my dick until I felt my nut rise. I grabbed my girl's plate off the counter and nutted on top of it. Grabbing a spoon, I mixed it up good so she wouldn't see it when she was eating. I covered her plate up and placed it in the microwave.

A nigga played slow, but I knew my girl was getting fed up with my shit. My daddy always told me when I wanted a girl to stay with me, I needed to feed her my nut. He said he did it to my momma and his daddy did it to my grandma. So, every time we got into an argument, I made sure to cook and add my special potion to her food. I would never let Egypt go. I would kill her and any nigga she tried to be with before I was without her.

I told Egypt it was until death do us part and I meant that shit. I fixed a plate of food and went in the bedroom to find something to watch while I ate.

Egypt

When I got home from work, Vance was laying in the bed, holding his stomach. I wasn't surprised, though, because every time he got sick, he turned into a big baby. He claimed the prison food messed his stomach up and now he got bad stomach pains.

I went to the bathroom and ran him a bath. I added lavender and peppermint oil to his bath water, dimmed the lights in the bathroom, and called his name to get in the tub. I went back into our room and got his night clothes out and laid them on the bed.

I was so grateful he had cooked because I was starving. I hadn't eaten lunch today in the cafeteria because they were serving sloppy joes and that shit looked nasty.

I headed to the kitchen to eat and wash the few dishes he used while I was at work. I grabbed a tomato out the refrigerator and sliced it up to eat with my chicken and rice. I noticed he had gone ahead and pulled the trash can to the edge of our driveway as well. Trash ran tomorrow and he was bad about waiting until the morning of trash day to move the trash can.

By the time I finished eating and straightening the house up, he was done with his bath and out the tub. I cleaned the tub out and jumped in to take a shower. When I got out the shower, Vance was still up, watching TV. I oiled my body down and put on my nightgown. I grabbed the massage oil from my dresser and got in the bed. I poured a little on his stomach and gave his stomach a massage. He swore my massages alleviated his stomach pains.

After a few minutes of giving him a massage, I got up to put the massage oil back on my dresser and washed my hands. I climbed in the bed with my back facing Vance and he wrapped his arms around me and pulled me to him. He turned my face toward him and tried to give me a kiss, but I turned my face away and the kiss landed on my cheek.

"Egypt, you know I love the fuck out of you, right?" he said. I nodded and rolled back over. I was exhausted, but Vance stuck his hands down my nightgown and started to pull on my nipples. He lifted my head and sucked on my neck. My neck was my hot spot, so my pussy got wet. He removed my nightgown and climbed on top of me, placing kisses all down my body, spreading my legs wide.

He nuzzled his nose in my bare pussy and inserted a finger inside of me. He finger fucked me for a couple of minutes, then took his finger out and sucked it. He removed his night pants and boxers before getting back in between my legs. He put his dick in my pussy and started grinding and fucking me slow. I tightened my pussy muscles and grinded against him. He shut his eyes and grunted.

"Damn, baby, this pussy so wet and tight."

"Fuck me, Vance." I fake moaned and made my leg shake.

He grunted louder and fucked me faster. Thirty seconds later, he nutted inside of me. I was on birth control, but he knew how I felt about him nutting in me. He cheated too much and I didn't want him throwing off my ph balance.

He fell off me and laid down with his eyes closed. I went to the bathroom to pee and push his nut out. I wet a rag with soap and water and went in the room to clean him off. He was already knocked out.

I put the dirty rag in the laundry basket and cut the shower on. My rose vibrator was under the bathroom sink, so I got it and got in the shower. I turned the vibrator on level three and placed it on my clit. It only took a couple of minutes to make me cum. I rushed through my shower and got out.

Laying in the bed, I wondered what was wrong with me. I was twenty-six years old and had never gotten a nut from sex. Sex felt good to me, but I faked the amount of pleasure I got from it. The only way I could cum was by using a vibrator.

Jordan said it was because none of the four guys I'd had sex with took the time to learn my body. She advised that I be patient and the right man would come along and fuck the shit out of me. I hoped she was right. I wanted the type of sex I read about in those good ass hood books.

I closed my eyes and let the darkness take over. The next day, I got up and got ready to head to work. Vance was still in the bed, asleep, so I didn't have to cook breakfast. I fixed a bowl of Fruit Loops to eat and left the house.

I got to work, and I only had four girls on my schedule to come in and talk with me today. The morning flew by, and everything was going well until I got a call to come to the girls' unit to try to stop a big fight from happening. I walked down to the girls' unit and there were five mental health techs surrounding a group of six girls. Two more mental health techs stood in front of another girl. I noticed the girl they were standing in front of was new and had just been placed in the mental health facility. The new girl was pretty and shy, and sadly, that made her a target for the other girls to pick on.

In all my sessions, I always told the girls how beautiful they were to help build their self-confidence and self-love. A lot of them grew up in households where they were neglected and were never told how beautiful they were, so they saw other girls they thought looked better than them and acted out in jealousy.

It took over an hour to separate the big group of girls and calm them down individually to stop the fight. The whole floor had their outside break taken for the day as a consequence for what happened.

I knew it would only be a matter of time before somebody caught the new girl by herself and attacked her. I hoped she fought back, though, because it was going to take for her to stand up for herself to get the girls off her back.

Five o'clock came and I was ready to get off and get home. When I made it home, Vance wasn't there, but I wasn't surprised. Most days, he stayed in the hood until late at night.

I was too tired to cook dinner tonight, so I went in the kitchen to make a sandwich. Whenever Vance got home, he could do the same. I took a shower and got comfortable in my bed to find a movie to watch, but was interrupted when my cell phone rang. The caller ID showed the city jail and I already knew who it was. I answered and accepted a collect call from Vance, telling me to come bail him out of jail.

Vance

Fucking around in the hood last night, I got too drunk. They got to shooting out there and the pigs showed up, harassing everybody. One of the rookie cops asked what my name was, and I told him to suck my dick. He got mad and arrested me for disorderly conduct. I didn't give a fuck because I knew I would be right back out.

When I got to the city, most of the cops knew me by name, so processing didn't take but a couple of hours. They let me use the phone after processing and I called Egypt to bond me out. After my phone call, they put me in the holding cell to wait on Egypt to get there.

When Egypt got there, she paid the five hundred dollars to have me released and they let me go. We did not make it home until almost three in the morning.

I promised Egypt I would pay her back the five hundred dollars when I got the money but she didn't even respond. I knew she was pissed that she had to get out the bed to bond me out, then turn around and get back up in a few hours to go to work. I could have gotten Keisha or one of my other little thots to bond me out, but I knew somebody would end up sending Egypt my mug shot and I didn't want her to get too suspicious and start asking questions.

I took a shower and got in the bed beside Egypt to get some rest. The next morning I woke up feeling refreshed and ready to make some money.

I got dressed and handled my hygiene. On the way out the door, I got a call about expanding my business and using fentanyl to increase the effects of my product. I had been trying to find the plug on fentanyl for months. A lot of the niggas from the hood were scared to add fentanyl to their dope because it was killing people. I didn't give a fuck who it killed if it was going to have the fiends hooked and make me more money.

I jumped in my 2016 white Honda Civic and headed to meet up with Chris. Me and Chris went and met with the plug on fentanyl. He fronted me four pounds of fentanyl and gave me a month to have his money. We went to the trap house and cooked up some dope with fentanyl in it to see if the fiends fucked with it. The fiends loved it. The trap house had been jumping all day.

After business was handled, I headed to the mall to look for a fit for the night. It was Labor Day weekend so I copped an all-white Ameri outfit and new Jays. I knew the hoes would be deep in the strip club tonight.

Egypt was off tomorrow, but I was not planning on coming home tonight. Keisha's freak ass had been sending nudes all day. I wanted to feel my dick in her ass, so I knew what the move would be after I left the club.

I left the mall and headed to this girl named Monica's house so she could retwist my dreads. A few hours later and me and the homies were fucked up in the club, throwing ones everywhere. I spotted Keisha, standing to the left of me, staring me down. I threw my head up at her and took my bottle of Ace to the head. Keisha must have been drunk as fuck because she knew not to address me in public. Tonight, she walked over to me and put her hands around my neck. I pushed her hands down and continued vibing like she wasn't standing in front of me, looking crazy.

Any other night, I would have slapped her in her shit for trying me in public like that, but I decided to let the shit slide tonight.

The DJ dropped that Lil Baby and I threw up my hood and started rapping.

"I be in the loop; she be in a group.

Brodie want her friend, throw 'em alley-oop.

Turned somethin' to nothin', bruh,

I'm livin' proof. How can I lose when we the who's who's."

Chapter Two

EGYPT

After I got off work, I took a shower and grabbed my Kindle to continue reading *Demon's Dream* by Elle Kayson. This damn book was so good.

I'd been calling and texting Vance's phone ever since I got home, and he hadn't answered. It was the weekend, so I knew he was probably at the strip club or a party somebody in the hood was throwing.

I set an alarm on my phone for four a.m. and went to sleep. At four a.m., I jumped up to turn off the shrieking noise coming from my phone. Vance's ass better be in his man cave because his side of the bed had not been touched. I got up and headed downstairs and Vance's man cave was empty, and I could tell he had not been home at all. I tried calling his phone again, but instead of answering, he sent a text message. He claimed he had gotten too drunk to drive home from the strip club and decided to crash at his Aunt Keisha's spot.

I tried to lay back down, but something was bothering me. I felt off and I couldn't fall back asleep. I tossed and turned before finally giving up and getting back out of bed. I decided to grab the keys to my black Tesla model 3 and go pick Vance up so I could come back home and fall asleep peacefully. I slipped on my house shoes and headed out the door.

Twenty minutes later, I pulled up to Keisha's apartment. Keisha was cool. I had chilled over here several times with Vance. Last year, he threw his birthday party here and me and her spent all day, decorating and getting everything set up.

I parked in front of her house apartment and got out. I headed towards her front door.

Before I could knock, I heard strange noises coming from the backyard. I walked to her backyard slowly and noticed she had left her room window cracked. I peeked inside the window and almost fainted. This nigga had Keisha naked on top of him, riding the shit out of his wack ass dick. I was so shocked, it took a couple of minutes to process what I saw.

I banged on the window and called his name. Vance pushed Keisha off him and jumped up, looking at the window crazy. I ran to the front door and started beating and kicking it.

"Open the motherfucking door!" I yelled, loud as fuck. Vance opened the door and slapped the shit out of me.

"Man, what the fuck is you doing? The police been hot as fuck in the hood all day and my shit is stashed here. Take yo' dumb ass home now!" Vance yelled.

"Nigga, I'm not going no-fucking-where. Why the fuck did I just see your aunt fucking the shit out of you? What kind of sick shit y'all got going on?" I screamed back at him.

I tried to push Vance's ass out the way so I could walk all the way in Keisha's apartment, but he pushed me back and blocked me from coming in. Keisha walked up behind him and started laughing.

"Stupid bitch, we are not really related. I'm just eight

years older than him and you dumb enough to believe every-thing this nigga tell you," she said.

"You a grimy hoe," I told Keisha's nasty ass.

"But yo' nigga love it. He spends more time over here than he does at home with you," she said, still laughing. I kicked Vance in the balls, and he crouched down to grab hold of them.

As soon as his head moved out my way, I punched Keisha in her face for all that slick shit she had coming out her mouth. She acted like she wanted to run up, but Vance pushed her ass to the floor.

Hoe started talking about when she caught me it was up, but I laughed and told her ass wasn't no pussy in my blood. I pushed Vance again, trying to get in the apartment and he reached back and punched me in my face. My lip started to bleed. He hit me so hard in my lip, my eyesight became blurry.

I ran back to my Tesla and jumped in, rushing home so I could start packing. I could not believe what the fuck had just happened. This nigga had punched me in my shit because he got caught up at a hoe's house that he told me was his fucking auntie. Who the fuck lies about some shit like that?

I'd been all at this woman's house, chilling with him and the whole time, they'd been playing in my face. Fuck him and Keisha. Fuck this relationship. Fuck this house, he could have it. I was done with all this shit.

Vance

As soon as Egypt ran to her car, I backhanded the shit out of Keisha and dragged her by her hair to the couch. She cried and begged me to let her go. If I didn't have my dope in her house, I would have let Egypt whoop her ass. I went to her room to get dressed, grabbed my nine I had under the pillow, and went back into the living room.

"Bitch, if you ever try to be funny with Egypt again, I will kill you" I told Keisha walking out the door.

She was still sitting on the couch, crying, but I couldn't care less. Keisha's only position in my life was to fuck me and hide my stash. I really should have beat her ass because if she hadn't left the window cracked, Egypt would have never heard us fucking.

I jogged to my Honda and hopped in. I sped on the highway and made it to the house in ten minutes. Walking in the house, I noticed Egypt had her suitcase and a big, pink bag by the door. I went to the kitchen and grabbed a kitchen knife, then walked back outside. I used the kitchen knife to stab a hole in all four tires on Egypt's car, then went back in the house and put the knife back where I got it from.

I walked to the door and grabbed the suitcase and bag. Egypt's ass had kicked me out plenty of times, but she had never packed her own stuff and tried to leave.

I walked in our room and placed the suitcase and bag on our bed. Egypt sat on the closet floor, filling up another suitcase with shoes. She was out of her damn mind if she thought she was leaving me. Hell, she wasn't even leaving the house tonight.

"You might as well put all that shit back and sit down so we can talk about what happened tonight," I told her and sat on the bed.

Egypt glanced up and said, "We don't have shit left to say to each other, Vance. I am tired of the lies, cheating, and abuse. At this point, you can have the house, but our relationship is over for good. I just want to leave and move on with my life."

"You not about to leave me. I admit I fucked up, but I promise I won't do it again," I begged her. She continued putting her shoes in the suitcase like she hadn't heard what I'd just said. "Egypt, I can't live without you," I told her.

"You don't have a choice. I am leaving tonight, and you don't ever have to worry about me anymore," Egypt said.

I expected Egypt to be crying or trying to kill a nigga, but I didn't expect her to act all calm. She didn't raise her voice, nor did she look mad. She really thought she could just leave me, and I would let her go? She must be thinking about being with another nigga. I wondered if she had been cheating on me this whole time. I felt my temper rising and I lost it.

I grabbed Egypt by her braids and dragged her out the closet. I kicked her in the stomach and punched all over her body.

"You told me you loved me and would never leave," I said every time my fist connected with her face. She screamed and tried to fight back, but it was useless. I grabbed her by her throat and started choking her. Looking her in her eyes, she began to lose consciousness. I reached over and checked her pulse. She was still alive, but barely.

I grabbed her cell phone and dialed 911 and dropped the phone beside her body. I ran to the car and pulled off quickly, headed back to Keisha's house.

Egypt made me hit her. She knew how much I loved her. I couldn't be without her, and I wasn't letting her go. Why would she pack her shit and try to leave me, knowing it would make me snap?

I pulled up in Keisha's driveway and walked inside. Keisha was still lying on the couch, but she had stopped crying. She was on her phone, probably texting her friends, being messy, telling them everything that had happened tonight. I grabbed her phone out her hand and stomped on it until I was sure it was broken.

"Vance, baby, calm down," she said, but I didn't respond. I grabbed her by her hair and drug her back to her bedroom.

"Strip," I said. She took off the robe she had thrown on when Egypt started banging on the window. She was crying again, but that shit didn't faze me.

"Get yo' dumb ass on the bed and put that ass in the air," I snapped.

She climbed on her bed and laid her titties flat on the bed with an arch in her back. I got naked and climbed in bed behind her. I rammed my dick in her ass and she screamed. I started fucking her in her ass hard. Her ass was tighter because I hadn't stretched her out. The more she cried and screamed it hurt, the harder I fucked her. When I felt my stomach tightening, I pulled out and nutted all over her back, then flipped her over and spat in her face.

I picked up my clothes and redressed. Fucking her wasn't enough to calm me down, so I was about to book a room for the night and smoke until I passed out. After I finished getting dressed, I headed toward the door.

"Baby, I'm sorry, please don't leave. I promise I won't say shit else to Egypt again, I swear." Keisha cried and ran behind me to the door. Hearing her say Egypt's name made me want to put a bullet through her skull, but the hood was too hot, so I turned around and spat in her face again and left.

I got a room at the Red Room Hotel and laid in the bed. I'd fucked up bad tonight, but I would figure out a way to get Egypt to forgive me. I wouldn't give her any other choice but to forgive me.

Chapter Three

EGYPT

God, why is it so cold, and why does it smell like rubbing alcohol? I tried to move but my whole body hurt.

Beep, beep, beep.

What the fuck is that aggravating ass beeping noise?

I tried to open my eyes, but I closed them as soon as I saw the bright lights.

"Doctor! Nurse!" I heard a woman scream. *Why does she sound so much like Jordan, and who is that crying?*

"Ma'am, try not to move," I heard a deep male voice say. I squinted and looked up at a man hovering over me. He was an older, white man with a mustache and a white coat on.

"Where am I?" I asked the man. My voice sounded like sandpaper, and my throat felt like it had been set on fire.

"Ma'am, you are in the hospital at UAB. Can you open your eyes all the way and look at me?" he asked.

"Lights too bright, throat hurts," I whispered. I tried to move around again, but I felt like I'd been rammed by a Mack truck. I wondered if I had gotten into a car accident and that was why my body hurt all over.

The doctor walked to the door and twisted a knob on the

wall. The intensity of the lights decreased. I opened my eyes all the way and noticed a nurse standing at the foot of the hospital bed. She was a Black nurse who was short like me. She had on dark blue scrubs and smiled at me. She had a warm smile that was comforting, and I would have smiled back if my face didn't hurt so bad.

I didn't know what all I was hooked up to, but I felt the catheter between my legs and the IV in my arm. My ribs were wrapped with something tight and it felt like something was on my head. I looked over and Jordan and Syria were cuddled together under a blanket on a small couch. They looked terrible. They were both crying, and they looked like they hadn't washed their ass in days.

"Pain," I said to the doctor. The doctor was an older, white, heavy-set man with a bald head and glasses.

He nodded and he and the nurse began to check my vital signs. A few minutes later, he told me I had been at UAB for eight days. Apparently, I was a victim of what the police assumed was a home invasion, but I had managed to dial 911 for help. He said I had sustained several bruises all over my body. When I came in, I had a black eye, my nose was broken, and my ribs had been fractured. The lack of oxygen to my brain I endured while being choked had caused me to slip into a coma. Luckily, my brain showed no permanent signs of damage. They had reset my nose and wrapped my ribs to help them heal. I would be in a lot of pain for the next couple of weeks because of the extent of the injuries. He was going to keep me for observation for a few days before releasing me on bed rest.

He told me he was injecting medicine into my IV and asked if I remembered what happened to me the night I was brought into the emergency room. I shook my head no. He told me it was common with head injuries to lose memories, and that sometimes the memories would all come back, and sometimes they would not. I nodded and he poured water into a cup with a straw.

My lips felt like they were cut from being so dry. I sipped the water and felt myself getting dizzy. I really wanted to talk to my sisters, but my eyelids were getting heavy. I closed my eyes and drifted back to sleep.

I didn't know how long I had been asleep. I looked over at the couch and both of my sisters stared back at me.

"Hey," I said to them. Jordan got up and walked to the hospital bed. She laid her head on my shoulder and sobbed. I felt terrible and started crying too because I hated to see my sisters crying. Syria remained seated on the couch, but she was also crying. It scared me that she was not talking. Now that I thought about it, I hadn't heard her talking when I woke up the first time, either. Syria was the baby out of the three of us and always had something to say.

"Syria, I'm okay. I am so sorry I scared you guys," I said, looking at her. My voice was still very raspy, and it hurt to talk. Jordan lifted her head off my shoulder and walked away to fix some more cold water to drink. I was so grateful.

There was a knock at the door and in walked two officers and a woman dressed in a black pants suit. I was pretty sure she was a detective. Jordan grabbed my hand, and I looked up at them, waiting for them to speak. I did not trust a lot of cops. I learned growing up in the hood that a lot of them were dirty, so I was always weary around them.

"Hello, I am Detective Thomas, and these two here are my colleagues, Jacob and Tim." I said hello to them. "Nine days ago, a call was placed to 911 from your cell phone. When the police arrived, they found you severely beaten and unconscious. Your front door was left wide open, and your car tires had been slashed. Do you remember any details from that night?" she asked.

I shook my head, no, and said, "No, ma'am, I don't

remember anything." I honestly did not remember any details and I did not know how I ended up in the hospital.

"In your bedroom, where you were attacked, there were two suitcases and a bag full of items on your bed, as if you were planning on taking a trip somewhere or moving. Were you about to move, or did you have a trip planned that you can recall?" she asked.

I frowned and said, "No, ma'am, not that I can recall."

"One last question. Your boyfriend, Mr. Vance Powell, has a history of violence. He pled guilty to manslaughter after all four of the state's witnesses recanted their testimony about him being the murderer in a double homicide that happened in broad daylight. Has Mr. Powell ever been abusive toward you?" she asked, staring at me closely. As soon as she said Vance's name, memories of what happened that night came flooding back to me. *Oh my God, what have I got myself into? He really tried to kill me.*

Syria got up from off the couch and walked over to the hospital bed. She leaned down and wiped the tears that rolled down my face. I did not even know I had started crying again.

The detective must have taken my reaction to her last question as confirmation that Vance was the one who had assaulted me.

"Ma'am, we can protect you. I just need you to tell me what happened," she said and walked closer to me.

I shook my head, no, and told her, "I am sorry, ma'am, but I do not have any helpful information." My daddy didn't raise a fool and I knew snitching came with consequences. I felt like my heart was about to burst out my chest. I grabbed my chest and tried to calm down. Syria looked up at the detective and officers and told them I was done answering questions. If I remembered any more details from my attack, we would have our attorney reach out to make an appointment.

I turned away from the detective and stared at the wall. She watched for a few more seconds before she and the officers turned and walked out the room.

As soon as they left, I broke down crying. I kept having flashbacks of him punching and kicking me. I remembered looking up at his face while he beat me and seeing it morph into a monster.

I looked at my sisters and knew their lives were in danger because of me. He always told me he would never let me leave him, and if I did, everybody around me would suffer. I told my sisters about everything that had happened the night Vance assaulted me and they were shocked.

"So, you telling me the woman he been calling his aunt this whole time is really one of the bitches he was fucking?" Syria asked.

"Yes, they had been lying to my face this whole time. She has to be around forty years old, so I never questioned it when he told me they were related to each other," I told her.

"When I catch that bitch Keisha, I'ma do her dirty," said Jordan.

"No, Jordan, I already rocked her in her shit. She's not worth fighting. Fuck them," I told Jordan. I knew if one of my sisters saw her out in public, they would do her dirty just like they'd said.

"I never liked Vance, but I would have never imagined he would do this to you. Times like this is when I wish our father was still alive," Syria said.

"Or that our uncles weren't serving life sentences because they would have killed his ass," said Jordan.

My father probably would have beat him up like he beat me up, but he would have left him alive. My uncles would have killed him without any questions asked.

After we lost our mother, we didn't have a lot of females around us growing up. My uncles stepped up to help raise us.

They used to wake us up early in the morning to drop down and give them fifty push-ups. They taught us how to box and would let everybody in the hood know not to fuck with us.

I remember one Fourth of July, we were in the hood, chilling with our uncles, watching everybody shoot fireworks. There was this one guy who kept shooting a roman candle close by where we were standing. One of my uncles told him to chill out and to aim it somewhere else but he didn't listen. He shot another roman candle our way and it almost hit Syria in the face. My uncles went crazy. They pistol whipped the dude right there in front of everybody.

Later that day, our father told us the dude had to have over twenty staples put in his head. It was my first time seeing something so violent and I doubt I would ever forget it.

They moved to Texas a few years after that and ended up with a murder charge. They got life in prison without a chance of parole.

The nurse came in the room and put more medicine in my IV. The last thing I remembered was staring at my sisters, knowing I had to figure out how to protect us from the monster I'd let in my life.

Grey

"Good morning," Mr. William, my secretary said, as I entered my office building. I owned three security companies located in Birmingham, Mobile, and Huntsville, Alabama. Birmingham was where my main office was located and I had managers overseeing the other two companies. All three of my companies had a stellar reputation.

Majority of the people I hired were either ex-military or business associates I'd met in my other line of work. Everybody I hired was put through rigorous training and testing because my clientele included a lot of politicians and celebrities. I took my clients' safety very serious and I didn't hesitate firing anybody who put my company's reputation in jeopardy.

"Your brother is in your office, waiting on you." My secretary smiled and looked me up and down. I frowned and nodded. I knew my secretary had a crush on me and my brother. He told me she approached him one afternoon while he was leaving my office, trying to get his number. She only had one time to approach me wrong and her ass was fired. She wasn't an ugly woman, but I liked my women with melanin.

I believe she was in her late twenties or early thirties, had blonde hair, green eyes, and a nice shape. She probably was used to men running behind her, but I barely paid her ass any attention. I never had a problem getting pussy and I had a phone full of bitches I could fuck anytime I wanted.

I was six feet four inches and weighed around two hundred and twenty pounds. I was born with a condition called heterochromia, which caused me to have one light brown eye and one pale blue eye. Me and my brother, Black, never met our father, but we knew he had to be mixed with something because of our skin color. We both had a dark olive skin complexion.

Our mother was the prettiest woman I'd ever met. She was dark skinned with light brown eyes that glowed when she got happy or mad. As beautiful as she was, though, she wasn't shit.

Black and I moved around the hood a lot growing up because every time she got a new boyfriend, she disappeared and left us to stay with family or friends of the family.

When I was sixteen, she popped back up for a few months with a nigga named Zade. Zade was about six feet tall, dark skinned, and wore glasses. They only dated a few months before she ran off again and we hadn't seen her since.

I walked into my office and sat behind my desk. My office

was huge with an open view so I could stand at my window and look over Birmingham. My interior decorator had done a great job with my request to keep things simple, but make sure everything she purchased was top of the line. I glanced at my brother sitting on one of my office couches and I could tell by the nervous look on his face, my mood was about to sour. I didn't know what he wanted, but he could take his goofy ass on somewhere and let me enjoy my day.

"Bro, you will never guess who reached out to me last night," he said.

"Who?" I asked, even though I didn't care who called him or what they wanted.

"Jordan hit me up last night. You know when me and her broke up, she moved to Tuscaloosa with her sisters. I never thought I would hear her voice again," Black said.

My brother had been in love with Jordan since he grew hair on his balls. We all went to school together, but I just spoke and kept it moving. She had two younger sisters who used to be everywhere with her, but I never paid attention to them.

Black and Jordan dated on and off for years, but Black could not stay faithful. She finally got tired of his shit and up and disappeared on his ass.

"Okay, so why you here, Black? What do you want?" I asked. He knew I hated small talk.

"Jordan called me crying about how her sister is in the hospital. Her boyfriend beat her up bad. She asked me if I could get security for her and her sisters. Their father passed from a heart attack a few years ago and both of their uncles are serving time so they don't have anybody to protect them.

"You know how much I love Jordan. I will kill a nigga and do the time with no problem behind her. I don't want some random ass nigga from your company watching over them, though. I'ma let Jordan and Syria stay with me, but I want

Egypt to stay with you. She is the one who is in the most danger. I know you will not let anything happen to her. You are the best brother and man I know. Please, brother, I am begging you for this one favor.

"Let her stay with you for a couple weeks until I can locate her psycho ex and handle that," Black begged. I stared at my brother for a minute. My brother had never begged for anything in his life. Hell, he never had to. I saw how serious he was, and I knew how he felt about Jordan.

"I will babysit Shawty for you," I told him. Relief flashed on his face, and he got up to hug me.

He said he was leaving to inform the managers of his restaurants that he wouldn't be available much the next couple of weeks.

Black was the owner of a few restaurants, and he liked to check on them every day, especially his soul food restaurant because it stayed busy.

When he left, I thought about his favor. I had never had a female stay with me before. I didn't do relationships, I just fucked and dipped. But as long as Shawty wasn't grimy, I was sure I could last a couple weeks watching over her.

I texted this girl I was fucking named Nene and told her to be waiting for me naked when I got off work. She told me would. I put my phone down and focused on the tasks I had to do.

The rest of the workday passed by smoothly, with no interruptions. I left my office about six and headed home to shower and change into a jogging suit. I grabbed thirty thousand dollars out the safe and put it inside my hoodie.

An hour later, I pulled up at Nene's crib, got out, and walked up to the front door. I pressed the doorbell and she came to the door with nothing on like I'd asked her.

Nene was a bad ass bitch. She was about five feet four, skin the color of caramel, and slim-thick with good ass pussy.

"Hey, Daddy," she purred.

"Man, chill with that daddy shit," I told her and walked into her house.

She knew I didn't like to waste time, so she closed the door behind me and dropped to her knees in front of me. She pulled my jogging pants and briefs down and took out my ten-inch dick. She placed my dick in her mouth and sucked it. I grabbed a handful of her hair and fucked her face.

When I felt my dick swelling, I took it out of her mouth.

"Bend over and touch your toes," I told her. She got up and bent over like I said, with her legs spread wide so I could look at her pussy. I reached in between her legs to rub her clit. I rubbed her clit until she came and moved my hand. I needed her pussy wet enough for me to fit my dick all the way in her.

I took a condom out my hoodie and put it on. Pushing my dick inside of her, she moaned and tried to run. Holding her hips to keep her from moving, I continued to push my dick inside of her.

"Stop running and take this dick," I said and started hitting her with long strokes. After a minute of long stroking her pussy, I sped up and started pounding her shit.

"Oh fuck, Grey, I'm about to cum!" she screamed and released all over my dick. I kept the same pace, then sucked my thumb and stuck it in her ass. I felt her pussy tightening again and knew I was about to pull another nut out of her. I fucked her ass with my thumb the same pace I fucked her pussy with my dick.

"Oh, fuck! Ohhh, fuckkk!" She moaned. She shook and came on my dick again. She was so loud, I knew the neighbors heard us fucking. I sped my pace up to catch my nut.

A couple minutes later, I released in the condom and pulled out of her. Taking the condom off, I tied the end of it, pulled my jogging pants and briefs back up, then walked into her bathroom to flush the condom and wash my hands.

Back in the living room, I sat on the couch and waited for her to go to the bathroom to handle her business. When she walked back in, she tried to sit on my lap, but I moved her to the side and turned to look her in the face.

"Do you remember what I told you when we first started fucking around?" I asked, and she shook her head no.

"So, you don't remember me telling you I only fucked with a female for a few months, then I ended the situation and moved on?"

"But I don't want us to stop fucking, Grey. I don't care what you do or who else you fucking, I just don't want our arrangement to end," Nene said.

I shook my head, no, reached into my hoodie and pulled out three stacks of ten thousand dollars bundled together.

"Here, Shawty, this is for you. I hope you have a good life," I said, handing her the money and standing to leave. She took the money but started crying and begging me not to leave. I continued walking out her front door and to my car. When I got in the car, I blocked her number and pulled off.

I always told the females I fucked what to expect. I never fucked with a female more than a few months before I ended it and moved on to the next. If they caught feelings, that was on them because I told them all I wanted to do was fuck. The money I gave them at the end was my way of thanking them for their service.

Vance:

I had been calling and texting Egypt's phone all week. I wanted to see her in the hospital, but I knew her sisters were there, and they already didn't like me. Plus, I was sure the police had been sniffing around and I didn't want to run into them.

I had Keisha call her cousin that worked at the hospital and asked her to find out when Egypt was being released. Keisha had to cash app her cousin money because her cousin said she wasn't risking her nursing licenses without getting paid. Her cousin called her back a couple of hours ago and said the doctor was planning on releasing her tomorrow morning. I was ready for Egypt to be released so we could go back home together and forget everything that happened. This is the longest we have went without communication. I been at this room for almost two weeks and was tired of wasting money on it. The feds were in town, so I'd been staying clear of the hood. I wasn't worried about my name popping up in any investigation, though. The hood knew I'd be sipping REDRUM if a nigga mentioned my name on some snitch shit. I grabbed a Rello and started breaking it down. I smoked and then called up this hoe named Star and told her to come through. An hour later, there was a knock on the hotel door.

"Yo," I said, opening the door.

"Damn, nigga, you smoked without me?" Star said, walking in the hotel room. She had on some black leggings that had her ass jiggling while she walked.

"Get comfortable and I'll roll up another one," I told her. She sat beside me on the hotel bed while I broke another rello down and rolled up. We smoked half a blunt before I put it out.

I grabbed her by her head and guided her down to her knees in front of me. She pulled my pants and boxers down and sucked my dick. While she sucked me off, I thought about stopping to get Egypt flowers or some shit like that on the way to the hospital. I didn't even know what kind of flowers Egypt liked, but I could find a woman shopping in the store and let her pick some out for me.

I looked over at the alarm clock on the nightstand and it was already one in the morning.

"Get naked," I told Star and grabbed a condom from my pocket. I put the condom on and bent Star over on the bed. I loved a big ass and couldn't help smacking it one time before putting my dick inside her. I fucked her from the back for five minutes before nutting in the condom and pulling out. I took the condom off and pulled my pants and boxers back up. I went to the bathroom to flush the condom and wash my hands. When I came out the bathroom, Star had laid her naked ass on my hotel bed.

"Ay, you got to dip," I told her ass.

"I want to spend the night here with you," Star said.

"Bitch, I don't give a fuck. Bye," I told her ass.

She jumped up from the hotel bed and snatched her clothes off the floor to put them back on. After she got dressed, she stomped out of the hotel room, slamming the door on the way out. She was lucky I had to be up early in the morning or I would have slapped her ass for slamming the door. Nasty bitch didn't even get up to clean her pussy off after we fucked.

I went in the bathroom to take a shower and put on a clean pair of boxers. I lit the other half of my blunt and smoked before I nodded off to sleep.

Chapter Four

EGYPT

The nurse informed me I was getting discharged in the morning and removed my catheter. I was happy and scared at the same time. I tried to get my sisters to leave and get some rest, but they would not budge.

I had gotten up and walked around the hospital with them earlier today. My whole body was bruised and sore, but at least I could still walk.

"Let me help you shower and get ready for bed," Syria said to me. Jordan walked in the hospital bathroom and cut the shower on while Syria helped me undress. I saw my face for the first time yesterday and barely recognized myself.

Vance had been calling and messaging me, but I refused to respond. My sister said he'd been on Facebook, making statuses about how much he loved me and how we would be together forever. He was out of his damn mind.

While the hot steam from the shower surrounded me, I cried one last time. I promised myself I would not cry again, and I would figure out how to keep me and my sister's safe. If I couldn't keep them safe, then I would move away and start all over again.

I had never been far from my sisters. Our father raised us to always be there for each other. He made us do everything together and always preached to us the importance of having each other's back, but if I had to disconnect from them to keep them safe, then that was what I would do.

Over the two years of my relationship with Vance, he had never been so abusive. He had slapped me around a few times, but normally, he would only slap me once then walk away. I thought back to the day he first put his hands on me.

I was mad he hadn't gotten me anything for Valentine's Day, so I cursed him out and told him I was going to go out and find a new man. He slapped me and told me if I left the house that night, I would regret it. I was shocked, so I ran to the bathroom and locked myself inside. I heard the front door slam, but I was scared he hadn't really left so I cried myself to sleep on the bathroom floor.

The next day, he took me out to eat and apologized for his behavior. He told me he had lost his temper and would never put his hands on me again. He blamed me for making him snap with the comment I made about finding a new man.

I didn't know why I didn't leave or why I kept giving him chance after chance.

Maybe I should buy a gun and get lessons. I had never thought about killing somebody before, but I couldn't let him ruin everything I had built. I knew if I did pull a gun on him, I had to be prepared to shoot to kill.

Before I could think more about it, I heard a knock on the bathroom door. I must have been in the shower too long and my sisters were getting worried. I cut off the shower and stepped out to dry off and get dressed. I opened the door so my sisters could see I was okay while I brushed my teeth. When I laid back down, Jordan came and sat on the edge of the hospital bed. For some reason, she looked nervous, and I did not like that.

"So, me and Syria decided to get you some security until

we can figure out the best way to get Vance to leave you alone," Jordan said.

"No, I will not let y'all go broke, trying to save me," I told her. All three of us were financially stable, but we weren't rich, and getting a full-time bodyguard had to be expensive. Who the fuck had the money for that?

"It's already handled, Sis. I called in a free favor. Me and Syria are going to stay with my ex-boyfriend, Black, and you will stay with his brother, Grey. Grey is the owner of three security companies, and I trust Black. He says his brother will guard you with his life and you will be safe," Jordan said. I started to disagree, but instead, I nodded. Honestly, I was too tired to argue. We would just have to see how everything went when I got discharged. At least I knew we would have a safe place to hide that Vance did not know about. I also agreed with my sisters about staying with Black because I knew he would do anything to keep them safe.

My sister had to be really worried about me to call her ex-boyfriend for help. She had not said his name out loud since she left him.

Black and my sister's relationship was complicated, but I knew he loved her. Black was her first love and the guy she gave her virginity to.

Growing up, I used to think they would be together forever and end up getting married. Jordan got tired of all the cheating and getting into fights over him, however.

When I got accepted into Alabama State University, she said she wanted us all to move to Tuscaloosa together and leave Birmingham behind us, so we did. I didn't remember his brother, Grey, but I was grateful he would let me stay with him. Staying with him would give me time to try to figure out this mess I had gotten myself into.

. . .

Grey

Laying in the bed, I looked at the message my brother had sent about coming to get him in the morning and going to the hospital to pick up the sisters together. I wondered just how crazy this girl Egypt's ex-boyfriend was. If he knew what was best for him, he would find him something safe to do. If not, I had no problem showing his ass the error of his ways. I remember the first day Zade pulled up on me and told me to take a ride with him.

I was standing in front of the corner store, waiting on Black to get out of school. I barely went to school because the stuff they taught, I already knew. I wasn't worried about a nigga trying my brother because we had been in so many fights that niggas knew how lethal our hands were.

I debated getting in the car with Zade, but I was bored, so I decided to slide with him. We rode in the car for about forty-five minutes, just vibing, listening to the new Jeezy mixtape. We turned off the highway and went down this long ass road that led to the country. All I saw was old ass farmhouses and cows and shit. Zade kept driving until he pulled up to this big ass white farmhouse. The front yard didn't have any cows or horses running around like some of the other houses we passed on the way there. This didn't look like the type of house Zade would live in, so I wondered why he'd brought me all the way out here.

He pulled around the back of the house and pulled up in front of a red barn and turned the car off. I felt inside my hoodie and wrapped my hands around my switchblade because there were maybe only eight houses on this long ass road, and all of them were spaced out far so nobody would hear me if I screamed. If Zade planned on bringing me out here to kill me, he would be taking his last breath today.

Zade reached in the back seat, pulled out a black bag, and laid it in my lap. "Unzip the bag," Zade said. I unzipped it and it was a bag full of cash. I zipped it back up and turned around and stared at Zade.

I did not know what the fuck this nigga was getting me involved in, but curiosity kept me from pulling my switchblade out.

"In my line of work, it is necessary for me to be able to read others. The first time your mother introduced me to you and your brother, I knew you was different. Your eyes have a coldness to them that is rare but can be useful in my line of work. I am here to offer you an opportunity, but you must first show me you can handle what is required," Zade said.

He got out the car without waiting for me to respond and walked toward the front of the barn. I placed the black bag in the backseat and got out to follow him. He slid the wooden barn door to the side and we both walked in, past a cage full of stinking ass pigs, all squealing at seeing him. In the center of the barn was a white man, sitting unconscious, tied down to a chair.

I walked up closer to the man and noticed he looked just like the city commissioner.

"Nigga, what the fuck is this shit?" I turned around and asked Zade.

"This man owed the wrong people money, and they no longer want him alive. I could have handled this myself, but I been getting too many requests lately and needed to add someone new on my team," he said and walked past the tied-up man and grabbed a cart. He pushed the cart in front of me. "The bag in the car has 100,000 dollars inside it, and all you have to do is cut off his finger and slit his throat and the money is yours.

"The customer wants the finger as proof of completion. If you accept this position, I will train you and you will get paid after each completed mission. The only rule is, you can never tell anybody what you do. I kill for some powerful people who will do anything to protect their privacy," Zade said, standing beside me. I knew before he finished talking that I was going to kill this man.

I grabbed the scalpel off the pushcart and walked over to the unconscious man. I could have woken him up, but I didn't want to waste time listening to him beg for his life. Grabbing his left hand and placing it on his thigh, I cut off his index finger. He woke up, yelling and screaming. I took his finger, placed it on the pushcart, and grabbed the tape to cover his mouth. I was going to grab the army knife next and slice his throat, but he pissed on himself. I stared at him, disgusted, and decided to cut off all his fingers, then sliced his throat. I took my time and removed each one of his fingers and placed them on the pushcart. After I finished, I grabbed the army knife and walked behind the man. I think he had lost consciousness again because he was not moving.

Grabbing him by his hair, I lifted his head back, placed the knife under his ear, and pressed down hard. I sliced his throat from ear to ear. Zade watched silently the whole time, and when I was done, he untied the man and stripped him. I helped him pick his body up and we threw his body in the pigs' cage and watched them eat him.

He then showed me how to clean myself and the scene properly so there would not be any blood left. The clothes I had on, we burned and changed.

That day, I became a murder for hire. The rush I got from taking a person's life was indescribable. I had killed so many people, I'd stopped counting my kills after I reached fifty.

Egypt

"Okay, Mrs. Jackson, all your vital signs look good enough to discharge you today. In this packet is instructions from the doctor and medication he has prescribed to you. He also included a work excuse for two weeks.

"It is important that you rest and let your body heal. Take your medicine as prescribed, and if you experience any symptoms listed on the last page, please come back to the emergency room to be checked," the nurse said. She handed me my discharge papers and the doctor's instructions and walked out.

On her way out the door, in walked two men. One of

them was my sister's ex-boyfriend, Black, so I assumed the other one was his brother, Grey. I had not seen Black in years, but not much had changed. The air around him was different now, though. He seemed much more mature, and I could tell by the way he was dressed, he was making more money. Black's eyes were unique. I guessed some people would call them light brown, but they really were more like a shining gold.

I looked over at my sister and she seemed stuck. They stared at each other like nobody else was in the room. Neither one of them said anything; they were in some kind of weird trance. I didn't know if it was sexual tension or regular tension building in the room, but I cleared my throat loudly to grab their attention.

Black turned toward me and smiled. "What's up, Sis?" Black said to me and Syria. I smiled back and said hello, then turned my attention to his brother and paused. I had heard of people having two different color eyes, but I had never met anyone in person who had the condition. One of his eyes was a golden color like his brother's, but the other was a pale blue. He was very tall, and I could tell he worked out consistently. He had on an all-black jogging suit with fresh Air Jordans. On his right wrist was a diamond studded Patek watch that I could tell was expensive. Fine did not even come close to describing the man staring back at me.

Black cleared his throat and I blinked. "Ladies, this is my brother, Grey. I'm not sure if you guys remember him from when we were young," Black said. I shook my head, no, and said hello to Mr. Grey. He gave me a slight nod, but continued staring at me.

My sisters had taken my braids down last night, so I had my natural hair pulled back in a ponytail. The swelling on my face had gone down a lot, but there were still bruises I could not hide. For the first time in my life, I felt self-conscious and was worried about how I looked.

"Thank you both for helping us. I will stay out your way, Mr. Grey, and try to get this situation under control quickly," I told them.

"Lil Mama, I'm not married, just call me Grey, and you staying with me isn't a problem. All I ask of you is to keep it real and don't steal from me. I hate liars and I hate thieves," Grey said.

"No problem. Can we stop by Walmart so I can get some clothes and pick up my medicine?" I asked Grey, and he agreed. I did not know what it was about Grey, but he made me so nervous. He had a vibe around him that was mysterious, almost dangerous, but I didn't feel like I should be afraid of him.

We got everything of mine that was in the hospital room and headed toward the elevators.

Walking out of the hospital doors, I noticed a black Range Rover parked close to the entrance of the hospital. I followed the men toward the Rover, but I stopped when I heard a male calling my name. I knew that voice anywhere. I started sweating and shaking.

Grey grabbed my hand and led me to the passenger door of the Rover. He opened the door and told me to get in. I got inside the car and cried, wondering how the fuck Vance knew I was being discharged today. I dropped my head and prayed to God and my ancestors for protection. I prayed we would all make it from this hospital safely and away from Vance's psycho ass.

Vance

I had been parked outside the hospital for over two hours, waiting for my girl to be released. It took me almost an hour to make it from Tuscaloosa to Birmingham, where UAB was.

Every time a Black female walked out the hospital, I was ready to jump out my car until I noticed it wasn't her.

I looked up at the entrance again and saw her hoe ass sisters walking out with some tall ass nigga. Getting out of my car, I headed toward the entrance of the hospital. Behind them was my girl and another tall ass nigga, walking close beside her. I thought my eyes were playing tricks on me, so I yelled her name out loud in the parking lot. When she paused, I knew she had me fucked up.

The first guy I saw opened the back door of the Range Rover and her sisters climbed inside. He shut the door and leaned up against it. The other tall nigga who walked beside Egypt led her to the passenger side of the car and she got inside.

Jogging toward the Range Rover, I went straight toward the passenger side of the car. The first nigga mugged me hard as fuck. Nigga clearly had an issue, but after I got my girl out this car, we could get active. I rounded the car and stepped up to the other nigga who stood in front of the passenger door. These niggas looked just alike, except the one in front of me had creepy looking eyes.

"Man, Egypt, get the fuck out the car before I get mad!" I yelled loud enough for her to hear inside the car. I tried to get closer to the car, but this nigga stepped in front of me, blocking my view.

"Ay, homie, Egypt and her sisters no longer exist to you," this mixed ass nigga had the nerve to tell me."

"Pussy ass nigga, move so I can get my girl out this fucking car!" I yelled and pulled up my pants, ready to swing. He lifted his hoodie and showed me he was packing. I stared at him for a minute, pissed that I had left my nine in the car.

"Shit, say less. I'll catch y'all again real soon," I told that nigga and jogged back to my car. I got inside and grabbed my gun from out the glove compartment and laid it on my lap. If it were not for the hospital cameras, I would have lit his shit up like the Fourth of July.

I punched the steering wheel and watched the Range Rover pull off with my girl inside. I couldn't believe I had let some niggas catch me slipping without my gun. I didn't know where Egypt had met those niggas, but I was going to kill those niggas and make Egypt watch since she didn't get her stupid ass out the car like I told her. I wondered if she had been cheating on me with that nigga. She was too comfortable getting in his car for him to just be some random ass nigga.

I pulled out the parking lot of the hospital, seeing red. Egypt had just played the fuck out of me, but I would get the last laugh. I stopped by a gas station and bought a gasoline jug and paid to have it filled up. I put it in my backseat and headed back home to Tuscaloosa.

I swear all these hoes were the same. As soon as it got dark enough tonight, I was going to show Egypt what came with playing with a nigga like me.

Chapter Five

GREY

I did not give a fuck how crazy that nigga thought he was. That nigga had just signed his death certificate.

I kept checking my car windows to make sure he hadn't followed us from the hospital. My brother, Black, was trying to calm the sisters down and let them know we would not let anything happen to them.

"What's that nigga's name?" I glanced at Egypt and asked.

She whispered, "Vance Powell." She said it so low, I could barely hear her. She was clearly very afraid of him but Vance was a dead man walking.

I glanced at Egypt again. She was so fucking beautiful. Even with the bruises on her face, she was fine as fuck. There was something about her that made me want to protect her.

I pulled into the parking lot at Walmart and jumped out my car to open the door for Egypt. She was short,, barely reaching the middle of my chest.

It took her and her sisters over an hour to shop for necessities and to get her medicine. She said she did not want to go to her house to get her clothes and stuff because she was afraid he would be there. I told Lil Mama it wasn't a problem if she preferred to hit the mall to shop. She just shook her head no and continued shopping.

They tried paying for their own stuff, but I ignored them and handed the cashier my credit card. The females I fucked thought they were too good to shop at Walmart. I liked how she turned down my offer to hit the mall up and tried to pay for her own stuff. Lil Mama was beautiful and independent.

We got back in the car and headed toward my and Black's houses. We both stayed in Shoal Creek. Shoal Creek was the most expensive gated community in Birmingham. All their houses cost a few million dollars and up to purchase. They had 24/7 security, and a person couldn't enter without being with a resident or being put on the resident's list.

We pulled up to Black's house and I helped my brother with Jordan and Syria's bags. Black had been following Jordan like a sick puppy ever since we left the hospital, but she was keeping her distance. I didn't know shit about being in love, so I was staying out of whatever they had going on.

I could tell Egypt did not want to leave her sisters. They had to promise her they would be okay. It would have been impossible for my brother to protect all three of them by himself.

I only lived about seven minutes away from Black, but Egypt had fallen asleep on the way there. I wasn't surprised, though, because she had taken her medicine as soon as we left Walmart, and I was sure it had kicked in.

I got out the car and walked around to the passenger side to wake Egypt up. "Get up, Lil Mama, we here," I told her, shaking her gently. She woke up and looked around, confused, until she looked at me. I grabbed her hand and helped her out. She followed me and waited as I unlocked the door and cut my alarm system off.

I wanted to give her a tour of my home, but I knew she

was too tired. I had seven bedrooms, five bathrooms, a pool, gym, and theater.

As soon as we got to the stairs, she stumbled. I turned around and stopped her from trying to walk further. Scooping down to pick her up, I carried her in my arms.

"Grey, put me down. I can walk," she said, but I ignored her. She laid her head on my shoulder, lifted her hand, and placed it over my heart. I stopped walking and looked down at her. She had closed her eyes and her breathing was shallow. I felt something strange inside my body. I did not know what the fuck was going on with me, but I did not like the way I felt.

I continued walking up the stairs and headed toward my bedroom. I had planned on letting Egypt sleep in the guest room right next to my bedroom, but I walked right past it and into my room. I laid Egypt down in my bed and stripped down to my briefs. I climbed in the bed beside her and drifted off to sleep.

Vance

I made it back to Tuscaloosa and stopped by the liquor store before heading to the hotel I was staying at. When I got in the hotel room, I opened my bottle of Hennessy and started drinking. All I could think about was Egypt getting in the car with another man right in front of me. I was glad I hadn't stopped and bought any flowers for Egypt's ass this morning like I had planned to.

I put my bottle down and grabbed my cell phone. I called Egypt thirteen times, and she didn't pick up one call. I picked my bottle back up and started drinking. I felt like I was losing my control over her and I didn't like that.

I grabbed my phone again, but this time, I sent her text message after text message. I knew she would read them, even if she didn't answer the phone, and see how serious I was about her coming back to me.

I drank half the bottle of Hennessy and passed out. I woke up later in the day and picked up my phone, expecting to see missed calls or texts from Egypt, apologizing to me and telling me to calm down. When I saw she hadn't responded at all, I jumped in the shower and got dressed. I called Chris and told him I needed him to ride with me to handle business and to be ready at twelve.

When it turned eleven, I left the hotel and headed toward Chris's house. I pulled up at Chris's house forty minutes later and blew the horn. Chris walked outside five minutes later.

"What up, nigga?" Chris said, getting in my car.

"What up?" I replied.

"Where are we going?" he asked.

"I'm about to go bust all the windows out of Egypt's house and set her house on fire. I need you to take pictures of me doing it so I can send them to her," I told him.

"Nigga, what?" Chris said, snapping his head around to look at me. I ignored him and kept driving.

"Yo, you can't be serious," he said ten minutes later as we got closer to Egypt's house. "Man, yo' crazy ass about to get us locked up for arson," Chris said as I parked in front of Egypt's house. Her Tesla was still there, sitting in the driveway on four flats, and I hoped that motherfucker caught on fire too.

"Here," I said, handing Chris my phone. He shook his head but took it out my hand. I reached in the back seat and grabbed the gasoline I'd purchased earlier and got out. I placed the gasoline on the hood of my car and popped my trunk. I searched my trunk until I found the bat I was looking for and took it out. I grabbed the gasoline and the bat and walked to the front door. The police must have closed the door and locked the bottom lock because I remembered leaving it open.

I set the gasoline and bat down so I could pull out my extra key and unlocked the door. Me and Chris walked in the house, and I went straight to our bedroom.

"Get ready," I told Chris and waited for him to open my camera app.

"Shit, you might as well smile, nigga," Chris said. I swung the bat and busted the window out.

"Ay, you got that, right?" I asked Chris while I walked through the house, busting out all the other windows.

"Man, this shit is crazy," Chris said, instead of answering my question. I tossed him my bat when I finished and picked up the gasoline.

"Man, come on, think about this," Chris said.

"Fuck her, come on," I replied. I poured gasoline all over the house, then went in her room where her clothes were piled up on the bed and threw gasoline on them. "Get ready to run," I told Chris, and picked up one of her shirts out the pile. I took my lighter out my pocket and lit the shirt on fire. I threw the shirt on top of the clothes soaked in gasoline and we took off running.

We ran to the car and jumped in. The fire spread fast as fuck; it looked like half the house was already burning.

"You got the pictures, right?" I asked Chris as I pulled off. Chris didn't say anything, he just stared, shaking his head. I headed back toward Chris's house to drop him back off.

When we pulled up in his yard, I looked at the pictures he took and smiled. I chose three pictures and sent them to Egypt's ass. I bet she would start answering the phone for me now.

I headed back to the hotel with a smile on my face. If I didn't hear from her tomorrow, by the end of the day, I was going to do the same exact thing to both of her sisters' houses. Egypt was bringing her ass back to me and I wouldn't stop until she did.

Egypt

I woke up and stretched my arms. My hand hit a hard ass surface and I almost jumped out of my skin. Grey opened his eyes and looked at me. I started to ask him what the hell was I doing in the bed with him, but I remembered how bad my breath smelled in the morning before I brushed my teeth. I sat up in the bed and turned my head away from him.

"Bathroom?" I asked, and he pointed to the door in the room.

He got out the bed and I felt my pussy throb. Grey only had on a pair of black briefs. He had a tattoo of a Grim Reaper that covered his whole chest. The Grim Reaper had one light brown eye and one pale blue eye just like him. His arms and legs were bulky with muscles, but not so much that it didn't match the rest of his body. I lowered my eyes and had to squeeze my thighs tight. His dick looked so big, I thought his briefs were going to bust trying to hold it.

"Ay, Lil Mama, stop looking at me like that because this dick will ruin your life and I don't do relationships," he said, and it broke my trance. I was so embarrassed, I did not know what to say. This man probably thought I was a hoe after the way I'd just stared him down.

"Can I get the keys so I can grab the stuff I bought yesterday? I need to take a shower and brush my teeth," I asked him.

I heard him walking around the room and a dresser drawer opened. His room was huge, and all the furniture was black. A few minutes later, he walked past me wearing black night pants and a black tee shirt. He picked the car keys up off the nightstand and walked out the door. This would be my last day sleeping in the bed beside him. He was too damn fine.

I cut my cell phone on, and I had over fifty messages and voicemails from Vance. I opened the messages and all I saw were death threats toward me and my sisters. He didn't even know Grey and Black's name, but he was threatening to kill them too.

The last message he sent said snitches get stitches and it had three photo attachments at the end. I looked at the pictures he sent me and started rocking back and forth. The first photo was a picture of all the windows being bust out my house. The second photo was a picture of him setting all the clothes I had on the bed on fire. The third picture made me fall to my knees and start crying. He took a picture of my whole house on fire.

When Grey came back upstairs, I was still crying and rocking back and forth on my knees.

"Ay, Lil Mama, what's wrong?" he asked, but I couldn't get the words out to tell him what had happened. He took my phone out my hands and looked at the shit Vance had done. He picked me up off the floor, sat on the bed with me in his arms, and let me cry while holding me. He never said anything, just held me and let me cry. I felt like I had cried for over thirty minutes straight before I climbed out his lap.

I got my toothbrush and comfortable clothes out and headed to the bathroom to handle my hygiene.

In the shower, I made my mind up that I would disappear after I got off bed rest. I would not bring any harm to my sisters or Black and Grey. I would move to a small town where nobody knew who I was and start all over.

When I came out the bathroom, Grey had showered and put on a pair of black pants and a button-down shirt. He looked and smelled so good it was hard not to stare. I wanted to thank him for holding me while I cried, but I had no energy left to talk.

"I have to go in to work, but I put your medicine and a water bottle right here," Grey said, and I nodded. I walked to the nightstand to pick up the water bottle and took my medicine. He watched me climb back in his bed and close my eyes. I kept my eyes closed until I fell asleep.

I woke back up a couple of hours later and just laid there, looking at the ceiling.

Everything I'd worked so hard for was gone. He could have just bust the windows out and left, but he wanted to do more than just get my attention. He wanted to hurt me, all because I didn't get out of the car at the hospital like he told me to.

In the pictures he sent, he started the fire in my room, on top of my clothes. The only clothes I had now were the ones I'd gotten from Walmart yesterday. He made sure in every picture he sent, his face was in it. I wondered if I went to the police and he went to jail would that stop him from sending someone else after me and my sisters. I didn't know what to do. I had never been more afraid in my life than I was now. I cried myself to sleep.

Grey

It took every ounce of self-control I possessed not to say fuck work and look for Vance's bitch ass. Vance wasn't a man; he was a bitch. Only a bitch ass nigga would beat on a woman, then set her house on fire because she didn't want to be with him.

When I came upstairs and saw Lil Mama crying, I thought she was having a mental breakdown. After seeing the messages and pictures he'd sent to her phone, I knew I couldn't wait too much longer to kill his bitch ass.

As soon as I got in my office, I went to my safe and opened it. I took out my burner phone and called Zade to tell him I wanted Vance snatched and brought to the barn tonight. I would pay 250,000 for the rush job.

I sat at my desk and pulled my cell phone out. I opened my camera app and watched Egypt curled up in my bed, sleep. I closed the app and pulled my financial reports up on the computer and started working.

All day, Egypt had been on my mind heavy. I tried to stay focus but my thoughts keep going back to her. I wanted Egypt bad and that confused me. The way she was staring at me when I got out the bed almost made me bend her lil ass over. I don't want to hurt Egypt so I keep it real with her and told her I didn't do relationships. I could tell she was embarrassed but when I came back upstairs the moment was forgotten and she was crying over the messages she received. She been in the bed all day. I been checking the cameras every hour making sure she was okay. II stayed at work until about six, then headed home. When I got home, Egypt was laying in the bed, watching TV.

"What's up, Lil Mama? How are you feeling?" I asked Egypt.

"I'm okay," she replied, trying to give me a smile. I knew she really wasn't okay and was trying hard not to break.

I went downstairs and fixed us some tomato soup and grilled cheese. It was one of the few foods I knew how to cook without burning my house down. I carried the food upstairs to her and watched her eat, then take her medicine. She had fallen back asleep by the time I got out the shower.

I got dressed and left back out the house. Zade was bringing my package at nine, and the barn was almost an hour away.

An hour later, I was pulling into the house in the country. I drove around back to park in front of the barn. After tonight, Vance would no longer be a problem for Egypt, but I wasn't sure if I wanted Egypt to leave me yet. I had no idea exactly what that meant, and I didn't have the time to try to figure it out.

I got out my car and slid the barn door open to walk in. The pigs got excited when they saw me. Zade paid somebody to take care of them; I only came when I was about to bless them with a special treat.

My phone started vibrating and I knew it was a message from Zade, letting me know he was here. I grabbed my push-cart from the back of the barn and waited. A few minutes later, Zade drug an unconscious Vance through the barn doors. He brought him to my feet, and I smiled. I dapped Zade up and told him I would get up with him soon. He told me he had a mission he needed me on next week and I nodded.

Normally, I wouldn't mind Zade staying and watching me handle business, but I wanted some privacy tonight. I waited until Zade left and closed the barn doors before I reached down and slapped the fuck out of Vance.

"Wake yo' bitch ass up," I said and slapped his ass again. I told Zade earlier not to inject him with a heavy dose of GHB. GHB was my and Zade's drug of choice when we needed a target to be unconscious so they could be moved around easily.

After a few more slaps, he woke up. He jumped up and looked around the barn. He looked at me and pulled his pants up.

"Ay, ain't you the nigga that took my girl the other day?" he said and started walking closer to me.

I reached back and punched him in the same eye he'd blacked on Egypt's face. He fell in the dirt, and I continued punching him in his face. He screamed and tried to fight back but I didn't let up. I wanted to give him a fair fight, but hearing him call Egypt his girl pissed me off. I had blood all over my hands, but I kept punching him until he was unconscious and barely alive.

I got up and grabbed my blow torch off my cart. I burned him up and down his face and arms, leaving burn marks everywhere. I put my blow torch up and grabbed my switchblade. I cut his clothes off him and stabbed him in his chest a couple of times. I got up and laid my switchblade back down and grabbed my meat cleaver. I chopped off his arms and legs and tossed them to the pigs. I placed my meat cleaver at his neck and lifted it up and swung it down hard. His head came off and rolled in the dirt. I tossed his head to the pigs and bent down to grab what was left of his body and threw that in with the rest. The pigs squealed loudly, going crazy eating his body parts.

I stood there and watched them eat him for a couple of minutes before I started cleaning up my tools and burning the clothes.

By the time I made it back to my house, I was exhausted, so I showered again and climbed in bed beside Egypt and fell asleep.

Egypt

It had been three days since Vance had burned my house down and I had barely moved from Grey's bed. I changed my number the day after it happened and deleted all my social media accounts. My sisters had been begging me to let them come over and spend time with me, but I just wanted a few days alone.

My body no longer hurt every time I moved, and my black eye was gone. Grey had been so nice to me. Every day, he made sure I ate and took my medicine. I wanted to do something nice for him in return today, so I decided I would cook him dinner tonight.

I got up to take a shower and get dressed. I took my makeup out my purse and beat my face. It took forever to untangle my hair and brush it into a more decent-looking ponytail. When I finished making myself look good, I felt a lot better.

I headed downstairs to his kitchen, which was something straight out a magazine. I opened the refrigerator and freezer, and they were packed with food. Dinner would be rib-eye steaks, home-made garlic mashed potatoes, and broccoli. For dessert, I would make a strawberry cheesecake.

I took out my phone to turn on some music and started cooking. It had been weeks since I'd last cooked, and I missed it.

"Damn, Lil Mama, what you got going on in here?" Grey said, startling me. I hadn't heard him come in.

"Hey, I hope you don't mind me cooking you dinner," I replied and turned around to look at him.

"Hell naw, I don't. I'm hungry as fuck," he replied and chuckled.

Laughing, I said, "Dinner will be ready in twenty minutes." He nodded and jogged up the stairs.

"Grey," I called out twenty minutes later, and he jogged down the stairs. Grey went straight to his bar and fixed himself a shot of 1942. I wasn't supposed to drink with the pain medications they had me on, but hell, I deserved some alcohol with all the shit I'd been going through.

"I want a shot," I told Grey, and he fixed me one and came to the table. I fixed our plates and sat beside him to eat.

"Damn, Lil Mama, this shit fye," he said with a mouth full of food.

"Grey, slow down, it is not going anywhere," I replied and laughed. We ate dinner and made small talk, then I got up and took our plates to the sink to wash them. Grey had this fancy ass dishwasher but I'd rather hand wash the dishes.

"You want to watch a movie?" Grey asked.

"Umm, sure," I responded and followed him out the kitchen to the theater.

"I can search just about any movie you want, so what you want to watch?" he asked.

I smiled and said, "*Love Jones*." *Love Jones* was my favorite movie. Larenz Tate was so damn fine, I would drink his bathwater. A few minutes later, the movie started. I looked over at Grey because I felt him staring at me.

"Grey, stop staring at me and watch the movie," I said and sat back in the theater chair. He picked me up and placed me in his lap. I leaned back against him and got comfortable.

I felt something wet against my neck and I turned around to look at Grey. "Did you just lick my neck?" I asked, but he ignored me. I busted out laughing because, who licked somebody's neck and then ignored them?

It felt good to laugh. I had been stressing over my situation with Vance for days, and soon, I would have to leave everybody I love and disappear.

I felt Grey's dick get hard underneath me but I didn't say anything.

Me and Vance had only been separated a few weeks, and here I was, lusting over another man I'd just met.

When the movie ended, Grey grabbed my hand and led me back upstairs to his bedroom. I thought we would find something to watch on TV together, but instead, he went into his closet and grabbed clothes. He went into his bathroom and came back out dressed in all black. He looked like he was about to go hit a lick, but I minded my business.

"I got to slide out to handle some business," he told me.

I knew he had to be leaving to go see a bitch because it was almost nine at night. I should have known somebody as fine and rich as him had an ol' lady. Hell, he probably had an ol' lady and side bitches too.

I picked my phone up and looked at the messages my sisters had sent in the group chat. I should have never told them I saw Grey in his briefs and got horny. Those whores did not take shit seriously and kept sending different memes on the best way to ride a horse.

I was typing a response when Grey snatched my phone out my hand.

"Who the fuck got you laughing and giggling?" he asked and started reading my messages.

"Grey, you must have lost your damn mind. Give me my phone back now!" I yelled. He laughed at the messages in the group chat and tossed my phone back.

"I don't play about what's mine, Egypt," he said, then turned around to walk out the room. Who the fuck was his, and what the hell was wrong with him?

Grey's ass was sending mixed messages and I didn't like it. I decided it was best to get my stuff and move in the guest room next door because I didn't want to continue playing with fire. I also was not about to be in his bed, waiting while he went out and laid up with another bitch.

I laid down in the guest bed and promised myself I would never be another dumb bitch for a nigga again. I woke up the next morning in the bed with Grey. Why he'd come and got in the guest bed with me instead of sleeping in his own bed was beyond me.

I knew it had to be late when he got in because I got up to use the bathroom around twelve and he wasn't here.

I got out the bed and washed my face and brushed my teeth. I had a taste for omelets, so I headed down the stairs to make some. I cooked us both a ham, cheese, and veggie omelet and cut up fruit.

Grey walked in the kitchen, and I fixed him a plate and

set it in front of him. "Good morning, Lil Mama," he said, but I ignored him and sat to eat my food. I felt him staring at me, wondering if I was going to respond, but I didn't look his way.

"Thanks for the food," Grey said, but I continued ignoring him.

I grabbed both of our plates and went to the sink to wash them. I knew I was being petty by not answering him, but I was mad. He had no right to grab my phone out my hand last night. Then to leave and go lay up with a bitch and come get back in the bed with me was very disrespectful.

He was single and I didn't have a claim on him, but he should have gotten his ass in his own bed last night. He was sending mixed messages and I wasn't with it.

I headed upstairs and went into the bathroom. I stripped down to my bra and panties and looked in the mirror. Walmart had cute matching bra and panties sets, so I'd gotten them in every color. I would have to go shopping when I disappeared and get a whole new wardrobe, but I didn't want to think about it.

I was about to unhook my bra when Grey barged in the bathroom. He stopped and stared at my body.

"Grey, I'm naked, get the fuck out," I snapped.

"Damn, Lil Mama, you look good as fuck, but why you got an attitude with me? What I do?" he asked, still staring me up and down. I felt my pussy getting wet.

"So, you don't remember snatching my phone out my hand last night? Then you left to fuck off and came and climbed yo' big ass in the bed beside me like you don't have your own room you could have slept in!" I yelled at him. I was salty as fuck about him leaving and I could not control what came out of my mouth.

Grey smirked at me and responded, "Naw, Lil Mama, you not mad because I snatched yo' phone, you mad because you think I fucked off last night, but I told yo' ass I had business to handle. If I was going to fuck, I would have said that. I am grown as fuck," he said in a low tone as if he was trying to control his anger.

"Get out, Grey," I said, but he didn't respond, just stood there, looking at me.

After a few moments , I rolled my eyes and walked up to him. I placed my hand over his chest. I didn't know why, but feeling his heartbeat calmed me down.

He looked down at my hand, and the next thing I knew, we kissed. His lips were so soft and tasted like fruit. He reached behind me and unclipped my bra, grabbing my nipples and pinching them while sucking on my tongue. I couldn't help it, I moaned, and he made a deep grunting noise.

I knew we had just met each other and had no business fucking, but we were both grown, and I was too horny.

I pulled my panties off and reached to grab his shirt, which he took off. He picked me up, walked into the bedroom, and laid me on the bed. He removed his night pants and briefs. He had the type of dick you only saw in porn videos. It was long and thick like a cucumber.

He pulled my body to the edge of the bed and dropped to his knees. He kissed my pussy, then licked me from my clit to my asshole. He put his mouth on my clit and sucked on it softly for a few minutes before he stopped sucking and bit my clit. I screamed so loud, my whole soul left my body. I felt my pussy juices dripping down my legs. He sucked on my clit again and inserted two fingers inside of me, fucking me fast.

"Stop... stop! Ahh!" I screamed, trying to wiggle away.

"Shut the fuck up and cum in my mouth," he ordered. I felt a weird tingling sensation building in my body. I felt like I had to pee. I tried to stop it, but it came so fast. My body started shaking and I felt warm liquid come out of me.

"Yeah, squirt in Daddy's mouth," he said with his face deep in my pussy. He put his tongue in my pussy and moaned while tongue fucking me. I never got my pussy ate like this before. " Grey" I moaned grinding on his face. He started rubbing on my clit while tongue fucking me. I felt the pressure in my body building again. A minute later I was cumming in his mouth again. " This pussy taste so good" Grey said while licking my pussy up and down. He stood up and placed my legs over his shoulders, putting his dick in front of my pussy hole, and slid in slowly. I felt like I was being ripped in two. There was no way he was going to fit all that dick inside of me. " Spread your legs some more. Let me in" Grey said and I spread my legs wider. He continued pushing in me slowly until he got all the way in. He moved back and forth slowly. The mix of pain and pleasure felt so good I felt tears in my eyes. "Good girl. You taking Daddy dick so good." He moaned and fucked me harder. I grinded against him and moved my hips to match his strokes. He put his face in my neck and bit it.

"Oh God, Grey!" I screamed again. I felt that tingling sensation in my body building again, and I didn't know if I could survive it.

He stopped biting me and wrapped his hands around my neck pounding my pussy. He leaned over and kissed me. We sucked on each other tongues while looking into each other eyes. My pussy clenched his dick and I started trembling. He squeezed his hands tight around my neck and slowed down fucking me. My whole body shook and I screamed his name while cumming all over his dick again.

Grey

"Fuckkkkk!" I could not stop myself from yelling and nutting all in Egypt's pussy. This pussy felt so good, I didn't think I could have pulled out if I wanted to. Egypt had the tightest and wettest pussy I'd ever fucked. I could still taste her on my lips, and I wanted more. I could eat her pussy every day for the rest of my life. Pussy this good had to be illegal.

I slid out of her pussy slowly and bent down to place a kiss on it. I couldn't believe I'd just fucked raw. I hadn't fucked a female raw since I lost my virginity. There was no way I was putting on a rubber with Egypt after the way her pussy gripped me when I was up in it.

We both got up and went in the bathroom to take a shower together. She washed my body off, and I washed hers. I didn't know what type of voodoo this girl put on me, but she had me doing shit I'd never done before. Fuck all that no relationship bullshit I wasn't letting Egypt go. She was mine and I was hers. I don't think she realize just how quick things have changed for us but in due time she will see. We went back in the room, and I grabbed my phone to text Black and let him know I was good and would be staying inside with Egypt all weekend. Me and Egypt spent the rest of the weekend fucking, eating, and sleeping.

Monday morning came and Egypt wanted to spend time with her sisters, so I dropped her off at Black's house on the way to work. She told me she missed having a car and planned on getting a new one soon.

When I got to work, my secretary was waiting for me with a message about calling my realtor back. She tried to ask how my weekend was, but I ignored her ass and kept it moving.

When I got in the office, I called my realtor back and found out the building I wanted in Florida was a go. I was ready to expand my security firm into all the south and not just Alabama. I called my brother and placed the phone on speaker so I could work while I talked.

"Yo?" he answered.

"I'm sending you money to take the girls to get their nails and hair did today," I told him. He was silent for a minute then hung up the phone. A few seconds later, he called right back. I answered and put it back on speaker.

"Man, what yo' goofy ass doing, Black?" I asked him.

"Hell, the question is, what is going on with you and Egypt? Shit, what happens if Vance pops up while I'm out with all three of them?" he asked, laughing.

"The first question is none of your business, and the second question is, just something you gon' have to take my word on that y'all are very safe and won't be bothered," I responded. Black got quiet for a minute , probably trying to process what I was telling him.

"Can we stop by and check on my restaurants?" he asked..

"You can do whatever y'all want, but keep your newfound knowledge of safety to yourself," I said and hung up the phone. I knew he wanted to question me, but I would never tell him what I he wanted to know.

I had a mission to go on Friday, and it required traveling and staying overnight to handle my assignment. I couldn't tell Egypt where I was going and what I was doing, so I knew this would play out bad. I could tell her I would be going out of town to handle business, but I knew she was going to be curious and ask questions I couldn't answer. My lil mama was going to be pissed at me, but I would make it up because us not being together wasn't an option.

I was so happy to see my sisters. I gave them both a hug and we went to sit down in Black's dining room.

"What's going on?" Jordan asked. I knew that was going to be the first thing out her mouth. I had told them I had something to tell them, but I wanted to wait until we were face to face.

"Don't freak out," I said to them. Neither one agreed to not freak out. "The day we left the hospital, Vance went and busted all the windows out of the house and then set my house on fire," I told them.

"Girl, what the fuck did you just say?" Syria said.

"Yeah, he sent the pictures of him doing it to my phone, but that was over a week ago, and I haven't heard from him since," I said.

"Why the fuck you didn't call us when you got the pictures, Egypt? Do you think we need to go to the police?" Jordan asked .

"I needed time to process losing everything I owned, and no, I don't think we do. He hasn't bothered me since it happened so I'm taking that as a good sign that he's moving on with his life," I told them.

"A good sign my ass. Why the fuck are you so happy? What are you not telling us?" Syria asked.

I couldn't help but smile. "I'm happy because I been getting fucked and sucked on all weekend. I went from not having orgasms during sex to having back-to-back orgasms."

"So, you and Grey are fucking each other?" Jordan asked.

"Yes, we are. And before you start, I am grown and happy, so let me be." I could tell she wanted to say more, but she didn't. I was glad she didn't because I had no plans to stop sleeping with Grey anytime soon.

Me and Grey hadn't talked about what was going on between us but I didn't know sex could be so good. All my life, I'd been faking orgasms, and here comes this nigga, with a dick and tongue game so cold, I didn't think I wanted to ever let him go.

Before they could ask any more questions, Black came downstairs to tell us he was taking us to get our hair and nails done, courtesy of his brother. There was still a weird energy around Jordan and Black. I wanted to ask my sister what was going on with them, but I could tell they still had unresolved issues. Jordan was mean as a rattlesnake, so she'd probably been taking Black's ass through hell.

Black took us to get our nails and hair done. We found a salon that did both and I got my hair braided in two Ghana braids going straight down my back. I decided to get my nails in the coffin shape and painted black. I think black was Grey's favorite color.

I kept looking around, expecting to see extra security because Grey told us he did not want Black out by himself with all three of us. I was scared that Vance would pop up and ruin the fun I was having with my sisters.

After we finished getting our nails and toes done, Black took us by to check on his restaurant. The restaurant we went to was called "Good Soul" and there was barely anywhere left to sit. I had heard how good the food was here, but I never knew it was Black's spot.

We all sat down to eat lunch when Black asked why I had been walking with a limp all day. My sisters burst out laughing and I shot him a bird for trying to be fucking funny.

I ordered a plate with pot roast over a bed of rice, macaroni and cheese, and yams. The way I'd been eating lately, I knew I needed to get back in the gym asap.

I started eating and joking around with my sisters when I felt somebody standing behind me. I turned around and it was Keisha's hoe ass, standing there with some girl.

"Where is my baby daddy at?" she yelled all loud and shit.

"Girl, lower your fucking tone speaking to me. And who yo' baby daddy?" I snapped back with an attitude.

"Vance, duh, bitch. Nobody has seen him all week, and I know you done talked to him," she replied, rubbing her stomach.

"Call my sister another bitch and see what happens," Syria said. Keisha mugged my sisters, but she didn't say shit to them. I was glad she hadn't because I couldn't stop them if they got up and whooped her ass in here.

I stood up and started laughing. "Girl, I been getting dicked down all weekend by a real nigga. Fuck you and Vance," I let her ass know. Her homegirl smacked her lips like she had something to say, but she kept her mouth shut.

"Whatever, just let him know we are expecting when you do talk to him," she said and stomped off with her homegirl following her.

Black's silly ass burst out laughing as soon as she stormed

out the restaurant. I'd been sparing the fuck out that girl because I really did not give a fuck about her or Vance's ass to stoop down to her level, but the next time she stepped to my face with that bullshit, I was going to rock her in her shit again.

I wondered why Keisha hadn't seen Vance in the hood. He never stayed away from the hood long. He was probably somewhere, hiding out after setting my shit on fire. I hoped he wasn't somewhere in Birmingham. Maybe he got a new girlfriend and that was why nobody had heard from him. I hoped that was the case.

I texted Grey and asked him what he liked to eat from here and then ordered us both to-go plates for dinner. We left the first restaurant and went and checked on his other two. By the time we got back to Black's house, I was exhausted. Grey had texted and told me he was five minutes away. I was ready to get to his house so I could shower and relax.

A few minutes later, I hugged my sisters and told them I would message them before I went to sleep. I didn't want to admit it, but I had missed Grey while I was out today.

Grey pulled up and got out to open the door for me. "What's good, Lil Mama? You look nice," he said, kissing my forehead.

"Thank you." I smiled and got in the car. I thought we were going to his house, but he went in the opposite direction.

"Where are we going?" I asked him. He didn't respond to my question, but I didn't fuss about it. I was learning that Grey didn't talk a lot and he hated small talk. I didn't think he did it to be rude, it was just the way he was.

I sat back and enjoyed the ride. He was playing King Von and I loved King Von, so I started rapping. I glanced over at Grey and he smiled and nodded to the music.

We pulled into Land Rover Birmingham and I wondered

what we were doing there. Grey got out the car and walked around to open the door. He laced our fingers together and led me inside the dealership.

"Hello, my name is Blake. Is there something in particular you two had in mind to check out?" a cute white guy walked up to us and asked.

"Pick out a car, Lil Mama," Grey said. I laughed because I thought he was telling a joke until I noticed he wasn't laughing. I shook my head no.

Grey and I had only known each other for almost two weeks so there was no way I was about to let this man buy me a car. "What do you suggest? She needs something new," he asked Blake.

"Grey, you are not buying me a new car. I was going to get a new car soon," I told him.

Blake looked back and forth between us, clearly amused. "Ay, are you going to suggest something?" Grey asked Blake. "Sorry, sir, I would suggest the 2023 Land Rover Range Rover Velar SUV. It is popular among the ladies, and one of the safest vehicles we have in stock," Blake said to him. " Grey I can't let you get me a new car. That's too much. We just meet each other" I said to Grey. " It really doesn't matter how long it's been since we meet. You need a new car and that's what you gone get. Relax and let a real nigga treat you right" Grey responded.

Grey clearly had lost his mind. A part of me wanted to argue and tell him I wasn't accepting a new car from him and the other part of me felt like I deserved a man who put my needs first. I decided to shut the fuck up and accept my blessing. Blake led us to a sky-blue Range Rover. "You like this one?" Grey asked.

"Yes, I do," I responded, and I did. It was top of the line and very cute. Him and Grey talked over the features of the car and Grey told him we wanted to purchase it now. Blake took us in his office and started handing me a stack of papers I had to sign. I almost dropped the pen when I saw the car was 126,000 dollars. Grey was quiet the whole time while I signed everywhere my signature was required. When I finished, I handed the papers back to Blake and Grey handed him his black Amex card. Blake charged his black card and handed me the title to my new car. He told us he would pull my car around front to us, and we walked out his office. As soon as we got outside, I jumped in Grey's arms.

"Thank you so much, Grey. I am so happy," I told him and kissed him again. "You deserve the world, Lil Mama," he said and kissed me back. Blake pulled in front of us with my new car and handed me the keys.

Grey

When we got back home last night, Lil Mama put on some slow music and gave me a full body massage. After the massage, she climbed on top and fucked me to the beat of the music. We fucked for three hours straight until we both tapped out and fell asleep naked in each other's arms. I got up early this morning so I could have one of my business associates put a tracker on Egypt's car while she was still sleeping. Her safety was a top priority for me. My feelings for Egypt are deep and the thought of anyone harming her again made my trigger finger twitch.

After my business associate left I headed upstairs to take my shower. When I walked out the shower the bed was empty. " Egypt" I called out. " I'm making breakfast. It will be done in five minutes" she yelled out from downstairs. I smiled and walked into my closet to get dress. After getting dress I unlocked my safe and took out some money. I locked my safe

back and walked downstairs to the kitchen. " Good morning"
Egypt said while placing our plates on the table. She had put
on a tank top and some shorts. Egypt was one of those
females who didn't have to do much to look good. She was
just naturally fine as fuck. " Good morning" I responded back
and sat at the table. I placed the money on the table and
picked up my fork to eat. I ate fast and got up to throw my
plate away. " You chilling here today or going to hang with
your sisters?" I asked Egypt. " I want to relax today if that's
okay with you? " she replied. " Man chill out with all that. You
good to do whatever you want. This money right here is for
you to get you some new clothes or whatever you need whenever you feel like going shopping" I pointed to the money on
the table and said. " What" Egypt said looking at the money.
I said what I said so I headed towards the front door to leave.
" Grey what I can't take this" she said following behind me. "
Look lil mama, I got to get to the office. The money is yours
just like the car. Be good" I said. " What happens when I
leave. Will you throw the things you are doing for me in my
face? " Egypt asked me in a low voice. I turned around and
looked at her." You not use to a real nigga and it shows.
Anything I get for you is yours. I would never throw some
shit like that in your face. Don't confuse me with them niggas
in your past" I said harshly. She pissed me off trying me like I
was one of them lame ass niggas in her past and who the fuck
told her she was leaving. I opened my front door and walked
out trying my best not to slam it. She was calling my name
but I ignored her. I jumped in my car and headed to my
office. By the time I made it to work I was back calm again.
Egypt had the power to get under my skin easily and I don't
think she realize it. My cell phone rang when I sat down at
my desk. The number was blocked but I answered it anyway.
I had been getting blocked calls for two days straight, but
every time I answered, they wouldn't say shit. It was probably

one of the females I used to fuck around with. If it was one of them, they had to be calling from a new number because I always blocked every female number I fucked after I ended our arrangement. I deleted all the female numbers I had in my phone the other day. I didn't want anybody else. Egypt had all my attention and I don't plan on fucking up what we were building. When I got off work, Lil Mama was upstairs hanging up new clothes. All day I wondered if she felt some type of way about the disagreement we had this morning but she was all smiles when I walked through my bedroom door. She asked me was I too tired to go over my brother house for a couple of hours. I told her I was fine and didn't mind going over to Black's house. I took a shower and changed into one of my jogging suits. After I got dressed she told me they planned on playing spades. She asked me to be her partner because she said Syria couldn't play and she took winning spades very seriously. I hadn't played spades since I was young , but I was down, so we grabbed a couple bottles of Dusse and headed to my brother's house.

Black and Jordan were talking big shit about whooping us and Lil Mama wanted all the smoke.

We turned on some music and sat down at the table to play spades. Egypt and I ran a ten on the first hand and my brother and Jordan were hot. A couple of hours later, we had whooped them two more times and they had beaten us once. We were all drunk, clowning each other and talking shit.

After the game ended, I ordered pizza and wings. The girls changed the music from rap to some dance music. They danced all over the living room, making videos and laughing. Watching Egypt dance and have fun with her sisters made me feel good. " Egypt got yo nose wide opened" Black said laughing at me. " Fuck you. I see you watching Jordan every move nigga" I responded laughing. He stop laughing and that made me laugh even harder. It has been a while since me and my brother kicked it without discussing business and I was enjoying it. Me and him spent the next couple of hours clowning each other and drinking. The sisters was too busy having fun with each other that they barely paid us any attention. By the time me and Egypt got back to the house, we were so fucked up, all we could do was stumble to the bed and pass out.

Egypt

Wherever Vance was, I hoped he stayed because I was truly happy. The next few days flew by with me spending time with my sisters or relaxing in the pool while Grey was at work. We talked about almost everything when he got home and then had sex all night. I was scared to ask him what was going on with us because I was catching deep feelings for him fast. It would hurt my feelings if he wasn't feeling the same way about me. .

I'd reactivated all my social media accounts the other day and I had a few people inbox me, asking if I had talked to Vance, but I told them we hadn't talked since the day I got put in the hospital.

If I hadn't heard from Vance in another week, I was thinking about finding a new house or apartments to move into.. Staying with Grey was amazing, but I did not want to end up heartbroken, thinking our situation was more than it was. This was my last weekend on bed rest, I started back working next week and I am excited.. I missed counseling the girls and was ready to see them again.

It was going on five o'clock so I headed down to the kitchen and cooked me and Grey some dinner. He had been so good to me. Last night, we sat up and watched a movie on Netflix while he massaged my feet. The food was done a little after six. He should be getting home soon, so I wrapped our food up and went upstairs to shower and put on my night clothes. Eight o'clock came and he still hadn't made it home. That was strange because he always made it home by seven. I tried to call his phone, but it was going straight to voicemail. Maybe he had a lot of work to finish and he was running behind. A few hours passed and he still hadn't made it. I tried calling him over ten times. His phone was going straight to voicemail every time . I laid in the bed by myself all night and tossed and turned.

I woke up the next morning and he still wasn't there. If he wanted to go fuck off with another female, he should have just said that instead of turning his phone off. We hadn't established what it was we had going on, but he could have kept that shit real with me. If I had disappeared and not answered his calls, I bet he would feel some type of way.

I refused to ignore the red flags a second time around, though, so I got all my stuff together and left. I knew his alarm system would notify him that I was leaving, but obviously, he didn't give a fuck.

The only people I knew in Birmingham were my sisters and his brother, but I didn't want to go over there because I knew he would end up popping up over there.

I drove downtown to the Hilton and booked a room for the weekend. Monday after work, I would start looking for my own house or apartment. My feelings were hurt because I thought we was building something special. If he had just been honest with me and told me he was not going to be home then the situation would be different. After the trauma I went through with Vance, I wasn't about to wait around for an explanation when he could have called or text me all last night. Me and Grey had been up under each other every day and fucking every night for a little over a month. Regardless of us not having a title I felt like the respectful thing to do was to let me know what was up. I knew he wasn't hurt because his brother would have told my sisters and they would have called me. At the hotel I spent my day reading books on the Kindle app on my phone. My actual Kindle was in the house when Vance set it on fire and I kept forgetting to buy a new one. I tried calling Grey a couple more times throughout the day but his phone was still turned off. Whoever he was with must be important to him and I wasn't about to put myself in another fucked-up situation. I would just stay here until I found my own place.

He told me I could keep everything he bought me, but I didn't know how I felt about keeping the car and clothes. He gave me twenty-five thousand for a new wardrobe and I'd only spent five of it on new clothes and put the rest in my bank account. Night time came and I decided to run me a bath to calm my nerves.

Maybe I wasn't meant to be happy or find love because it seemed like every time I gave my all, I ended up hurt in the end. Another night was spent tossing and turning until I fell asleep. I woke up the next morning and checked my phone, still no missed calls or messages from Grey.

I knew his office would be open tomorrow so there was a good chance he would be back from wherever he disappeared to. I was returning the same energy, though, and not answering my phone if he did try to reach out to me.

Grey

I left work and caught a private flight to my destination. The target was a news reporter who was causing a lot of trouble for the wrong people. They wanted his death to appear like a robbery so I broke into his home and disabled all his cameras. A lot of times killing involved waiting until the perfect time so I sat down on his couch and got comfortable. Finally later that night there was some noise coming from the front door so I pulled my ski mask down over my face. When he walked through the front door I put my gun in his face. " Don't scream or imma send a bullet through yo skull" I told him. "Who are you and what do you want" he cried out holding his hands up in the air. "Go to your room and lay down in your bed" I told him. " Please don't shoot. My father is rich and will pay you whatever you want just don't kill me" he said. " Do what I said now" I replied in a harsh tone pressing my gun harder against his head. The target started walking slowly towards his room crying and begging for his life. My glock47 had a silencer attached so I wasn't worried about anybody hearing any shoots. He laid his head back against the pillow and I put my gun on the side of his head. " Please don't do this" he begged me. Pulling the trigger I shoot him once threw his brain and once through the chest. He death only took a couple of minutes. I trashed his spot and took all his money and credit cards out of his wallet. After leaving his spot I found a homeless man to give the money to. The credit cards had to be cut up and destroyed but I waited until I made it back to room I had booked at the four season to get rid of them. On missions I always used an Alia's name to book rooms but I always wiped the room down before leaving to be on the safe side. Laying in the hotel bed I thought about Egypt. I missed her and was ready to get back home so I can see her. The rush I got from killing wasn't the same this time and I knew it was because I was worried about her reaction to me disappearing. Zade taught me to never turn my phone on during a mission so I rolled over and closed my eyes. My private flight was sched-uled to leave early in the morning and we would be landing back in Birmingham by eleven. I woke up the next morning and handled my hygiene. After my hygiene was handled I got dress and headed to my flight.

As soon as we landed in Birmingham, I powered on my

phone and called Egypt to let her know I would be home shortly. She did not answer my phone call, but I wasn't surprised. There was a notification from my security system letting me know somebody left the house Saturday morning. Opening my camera app I looked all over the house but Egypt wasn't there. I placed a call and got the location of the tracker device on her Range Rover. The device showed up at the Hilton hotel downtown.

I walked to my parked car at the airport and jumped in, headed toward the Hilton hotel. When I got to the hotel I parked and walked inside. It was only one lady working at the front desk and I was relieved. Approaching the lady, I shook her hand sliding a few hundred to her. She looked at the money and back up to me. I gave her Egypt name and asked for her room number. She looked like she wasn't going to give it to me at first but I told her I was trying to surprise my girl-friend without giving myself away. She told me if anything happened to Egypt they had my face on camera and gave me her room number. Egypt was in room 594.

I headed to the elevator and pressed the fifth floor once I got inside. When I got off the elevator I walked on the floor into I spotted her room. It was almost the last room on the floor. , I knocked and waited. I knew her short ass would have to answer to see who was at the door because she couldn't reach the peephole.

"Who is it?" she asked, but I didn't say anything. She opened the door a little to peek her head out and I pushed the door open before she could stop me and walked in.

"How the fuck did you know I was here, Grey?" She had a robe on and it looked like she was naked under it. I felt my dick getting hard.

"Hello," she said with an attitude.

"Why are you here and not home, Egypt?" I asked instead

of answering her question. She laughed and shook her head. I sat on the chair in the room and looked at her.

"Look, you single and can do what you want, but I think it's best I stay here until I can find somewhere new to stay. I haven't heard from Vance in a while and I should be safe to get a new place," she said and I laughed.

"How the fuck am I single when we go together, Egypt?" I asked her. Lil mama was talking nonsense.

"Nigga, please. Since when did we start going together, Grey? And if we go together, why the fuck did you not come home? Why the fuck you cut your phone off? It's obvious you got an ol' lady or whatever she is to you, so why not just keep this shit real? Stop playing in my face, Grey!" She was so mad, she was screaming and asking questions back to back without giving me a chance to respond. .

I got up out the chair and wrapped my arms around her holding her tight. . She tried to push me away, but I held on tighter.

"Man, calm yo' lil mad ass down then we can talk," I told her.

"Grey, let me the fuck go and tell me the fucking truth. If you can't, then get the fuck out!" she said, and tried to push away again.

"Me and you been together since the day you gave me the pussy. I have not talked to or fucked another female and I don't want to. When I disappear, I am working my other job. My other job is just some shit I can't talk about, and you just gon' have to trust yo' nigga," I told Egypt and unwrapped my arms from around her. I looked her in her face while I untied her robe. I was right she was naked underneath it.

Egypt

He untied my robe like that ended the conversation, but he had me confused as fuck.

"So let me get this straight. Me and you been in a relation-ship. You not talking to anybody else but me. You have another job that requires you to disappear and cut your phone off but you can't talk about it and I'm not supposed to find any of this suspicious. I'm just supposed to trust you ?" I asked him not believing the shit coming out his mouth. " Yes" he replied nodding his head. He bend down and sucked on my neck. My pussy throbbed but I tried to stay focus.. "The shit you saying sound crazy as fuck, Grey," I told him. " I am crazy but real talk everything I'm saying is true" he lifted his head and said. He leaned back down and sucked on the other side of my neck.

I placed my hand over his chest to feel his heartbeat. He stopped sucking on my neck to look in my eyes and say, "Trust me Egypt." Looking him in his eyes I felt myself weak-ening. He looked sincere and I couldn't think of one time he had lied to me before.

"If you cheat on me, I am leaving. There won't be any second chances," I told him.

"You not ever leaving me and I don't want anybody else. Now shut up and lay back on the bed," Grey said. I took my robe off and climbed in the bed like he asked me too. " You so beautiful" Grey said looking my body up and down. He removed his clothes and my push tightened at seeing him naked. I felt like I was about to explode and he hadn't even touched me yet. He reached his hands out to grab my breast but looking at his big dick had me moving away from his hands. I got off the bed and dropped to my knees in front of him. I hadn't blessed him with any head yet, but since he had established we were in a relationship, I was about to get really nasty. " For real" Grey said looking down at me grabbing his big dick in my hands.

I kissed the tip of his dick and sucked on the head of it softly. I swirl my tongue around the head and then put it back in my mouth sucking it with a lot more pressure. " Damn" Grey moaned and that turned me on even more. I slid his dick farther in my mouth. I went down as far as I could go, making sure I gagged. Spit was filling up my mouth and sliding down my check. I gagged on his dick a few more times before he grabbed my head and pushed his dick all the way in down my throat.

"Man, fuckkkk!" he said while fucking my throat. I let him fuck my throat for about three minutes while I played with his balls. Tears ran down my face and spit dripped on my titties. My pussy was so wet I could feel my juices on my thighs. I loved giving head and Grey dick tasted so good. His balls tightened up in my hands, so I knew he was about to nut. I snatched my head out his grip and started jacking his dick while I took my time, sucking on his balls. He moaned and cursed, and that shit had me feeling high.

I lifted his balls and licked his asshole. He jumped but didn't stop me. I licked it a few more times before putting his dick back in my mouth and letting it slide all the way to the back of my throat. "Swallow." He groaned and filled my mouth with his nut. I opened my mouth to show him his nut on my tongue, then swallowed.

He stared at me for a moments before reaching down and grabbing me by my neck to pull me up. He pushed me back down on the bed and climbed on top of me. We started kissing and then he turned me on my stomach and lick between my ass checks. He stuck his tongue in my ass and I screamed. He put two fingers inside my Pussy. He tongue fucked my ass while finger fucking my pussy. " I'm about to cum" I whimpered shaking. He fucked me with his fingers faster until I nut all over them. " Good girl" Grey said moving his tongue and fingers. He spanked me on my ass five times, then kissed both of my ass cheeks.

"I want this good ass pussy from the back. Get right baby," he said and I got up and got in the right position. He slid his dick inside of me and grabbed me by my braids pulling my head back. He started pounding my pussy with deep strokes. I threw my ass back meeting him stoke for stroke. " Damn Egypt fuck me just like that" Grey groaned. "Shit, Grey! Fuck!" I moaned and started shaking. " That pussy get even tighter. Fuck. Come on my dick Egypt" Grey said and I came all over his dick. He flipped me over and got on his knees to lick up all my pussy juices up . After licking up all my pussy juices he stood up and spread my legs wide. He slid his dick back inside of me and leaned down to kiss me. I kissed him back while he slow stroked my pussy. " Ummm" I moaned breaking the kiss and moving my hips to fuck him back. He placed my legs over his shoulders and fucked me faster. I felt that tingling sensation again and my whole body tightened up. " That it's baby, cum for daddy one more time" Grey said hitting my G-spot. " I can't it's too much Grey" I moaned. Tears was coming down my face. I feel like I was about to pass out from the pleasure. Grey put his hand between my legs and rubbed on my clit. " Fuckkk" I screamed. " You can take it. Come on my dick now Egypt" he moaned and I started shaking. My eyes rolled to the back of my head and I released the best nut I ever had in my life. " Damn you such a good girl" Grey moaned and slowed his strokes down. He moaned again and gripped my hips tight. " Fuck this pussy so good" Grey said nutting inside of me. He let my legs go and I fell flat on the bed. He laid on the bed beside me.

We both laid there for a few minutes, trying to catch our breath before getting up to take a shower.

"I have never had a relationship before, Egypt. I just used

to fuck off, but you don't ever have to worry about me cheating or putting my hands on you," Grey said while washing my back.

"I really hope you mean that, Grey, because my feelings were hurt when you disappeared," I told him being honest.

" I told you, it was for work. It's just some shit I can't discuss. I need for you to trust me. I also need for you to be patient with me. It's gon' be times when you get frustrated with me 'cause I ain't used to expressing myself, but just be patient," Grey told me.

"I will. I wasn't planning on catching feelings for you but there is nothing I can do about it. I need for you to talk to me. I understand your other job requires a level of secrecy but I need some kind of communication instead of just disappear on me," I told him getting under the water to rinse off . " I got you" he replied ,and we kissed.

We finished taking our shower and we got out and got dressed. I checked out the hotel and we headed back to his house.

When we got back to Grey's house, I started taking my braids down. Grey had damn near snatched them from my scalp when we had sex earlier and they looked a mess. I guess I would be rocking my real hair pulled back in a ponytail tomorrow, but it was worth it.

After I finished taking my hair down, I got in the bed with Grey and went to sleep.

The next morning, we got up early and got ready for work. My first day back at work had been going good so far. Grey ordered me some red and pink roses and had them delivered to my job. I had them sitting on my desk and couldn't help smelling them over and over. He FaceTimed me at lunch to check on me and we talked to each other while eating. After we got off the phone I realized my feelings for Grey was more than just deep. I was falling in love with him.

There was a knock on my office door, so I yelled for whoever it was to come in. In walked the lady detective who had visited me at the hospital. She had on another pants suit and her wrapped into a bun.

"Hey. It's Mrs. Thomas, right? Please, have a seat," I told her, pointing at the chair in front of my desk.

"Yes. it's Mrs. Thomas. How are you doing, Ms. Harris?" she asked.

"Please call me Egypt and I am much better now, thanks for asking. How can I help you today?"

I hoped she wasn't here to question me again about who assaulted me because I was going to tell her the same thing I told her the first time she questioned me. "When is the last time you had any contact with Mr. Powell?"

I wasn't expecting that question, but I answered honestly.

"The day I got discharged from the hospital, he showed up while I was leaving and asked if we could talk. I declined his offer and left with my sisters to focus on my healing," I answered her. I wondered if he was wanted or in trouble for something. "Why are you asking me when's the last time I talked with Vance?"

"A couple friends of his reported him missing. They are saying he hasn't been seen in weeks. Do you know any information that will be useful in locating him?" Mrs. Thomas asked and stared at me like she did at the hospital to gauge my reaction to her question.

"I am sorry, Mrs. Thomas, I honestly have not talked to Vance and I have no clue where he could be," I told her.

She stared at me for a moment before smiling and getting up to shake my hand. "Thank you for answering my questions. If I have any more, I will reach back out to you. Have a wonderful day," she said, walk towards my office door.

"You too," I replied to her as she walked out .

I didn't know what Vance had gotten himself involved in, but whatever it was, I wanted no parts of it.

I texted my sisters and told them what had just happened. If Vance really was missing, I didn't have to keep looking over my shoulders and they were safe to go back home.

Five o'clock came and it was time leave work and head to Grey's house. I locked my office and said goodbye to everybody and left.

When I got to my car to open the door, I felt something poking me in my back. I turned around and there was a guy with a black ski mask pushing a gun into my stomach. " If you scream I will shoot you" the guy said. " Calm down. I think you have the wrong person" I told the guy holding my hand up. " Shut the fuck up and get in the backseat" he said pointing his gun towards the car parked next to mine. I got in and he got in beside me. Whoever this guy was he was too tall to be Vance. His voice sounded familiar but I couldn't figure out from where. I looked up and Keisha was in the driver's seat.

"What the fuck is going on?" I yelled at her. The guy with the ski mask hit me in the face with the gun and I passed out.

Chapter Seven

GREY

When I pulled up in my driveway, Egypt's car wasn't there. She told me she got off before me and would be heading here as soon as she got off. I tried calling her phone, but she didn't answer. I went in the house and called and got the location of her car. It was parked at the mental health facility she worked at. She probably had to stay later than expected. I figured she would be home by the time I showered and got dressed for bed.

I placed a call for Chinese food to be delivered and headed upstairs to take a shower. When I got out the shower she still hadn't made it. Another hour passed and Egypt still wasn't home or answering the phone. I had this feeling in my gut that something wasn't right, so I changed my clothes and grabbed my car keys. I got in my Range Rover and drove to her job. Her car was in the parking lot, so I parked beside it and got out. I walked inside her job and asked the receptionist if she could ask Egypt to come to the front. She told me Egypt had already left for the day. I told her thanks and walked back out to the parking lot. I knew something was off.

I pulled out my phone and placed a call to have her cell

phone number tracked. Her cell phone was showing up at some house in Tuscaloosa. I got in my car and headed to the address her phone was at. I wondered what the fuck she was doing in Tuscaloosa, and who was she with.

I called my brother and asked if her sisters were still there. He told me they were, but they were talking about going back home soon because a detective came to Egypt's job today and told her Vance was missing. I told him I would hit him back and called Zade and told him to meet at the address. I didn't know what the fuck I was walking into, but I was ready for whatever.

It took an hour to get from Birmingham to Tuscaloosa. When I got to Tuscaloosa I followed GPS instructions to get to the address I was looking for. I pulled up to a house in the hood. The house looked abandoned . I looked around and noticed Zade was parked across the street. I took the safety off my gun and got out. Zade got out his car and walked towards my car. I got out a meet him halfway. " What's good" Zade asked me. "My girl missing and the location popping up here. Something isn't right" I told Zade. " Shit sayless" Zade replied. Me and Zade walked up to the front door, and I used my credit card to open the door. The front of the house was empty. There were people talking in the back of the house, so we headed in that direction.

I didn't hear Egypt's voice, but I twisted the knob and peeked inside the room the voices was coming from. Egypt was tied down in a chair with tape over her mouth, crying. There was a guy in front of her, punching her in the face and a girl standing beside the guy, asking Egypt where Vance was and laughing.

Me and Zade snuck up behind them and placed a gun to the backs of both of their heads.

"Don't say shit," I said before one of them could scream.. Zade hit the girl over the head to knock her out, then turned his gun on the guy in front of me. "Please don't hurt me. It's just a big misunderstanding," the guy begged.

He should have saved his last breath, praying for his soul. I tucked my gun in my pants and pulled my switchblade out. I stabbed the guy in the neck three times. He fell on the floor, shaking and bleeding everywhere. He was gasping for air but I knew he would choke on his own blood and be dead in five minutes.

"What you want to do with her?" Zade asked, pointing to the knocked-out girl on the floor. I walked over to her and stabbed her ass in the neck three times too.

Zade pulled out his phone to call the clean-up crew while I untied Egypt. I removed the tape from her mouth. " Stay quiet" I told her and she nodded her head. I doubted anybody overheard me killing them. If somebody did hear any commotion they would keep it moving. The people in the hood knew to mind their business.

It took the clean-up crew Zade called about ten minutes to get there. The whole time, I felt Egypt staring at me, but I didn't want to look at her. Her face was fucked up and I could hear her whimpering trying not to cry out loud. I was supposed to protect her, and I'd slipped up and let her get kidnapped.

She had also now seen a side of me tonight that I wanted to keep away from her. Shit was all fucked up.

" Imma stay while they clean. Y'all get out of here" Zade told me. " We good" I asked him. " Yeah imma make sure everything is handled properly and without a trace" he replied. I dapped him up and grabbed Egypt hand to walk out the door. On the way outside I looked around but I didn't see anybody watching us or the house. Zade would make sure they cleaned up right and go with them while they disposed of the two bodies. I made a mental note to send him some money to pay for the clean-up crew. I helped Egypt get in the car and put her seat belt on. She was quiet the whole ride back to my house. When we got home, I went to my bathroom to start Egypt a bath. Looking at her face had me wishing I could those two motherfuckers back to life to kill them slowly.

I took Egypt's clothes off and put them in a bag so I could deal with them in the morning.

"I am sorry I didn't protect you, Egypt . I promise I won't let anybody else harm you again," I told her. She started sobbing while I bath her. " Who was those people who kidnapped you" I asked her. " It was Vance best friend and the girl I caught him cheating on me with. They said Vance ran off on the plug and the plug was threatening to kill them. I tried telling them I didn't know where Vance was but they would listen. He just keep hitting me" she cried. " It's okay baby" I told her and helped her out the tub. I dried her off and put her in the bed. She still had a few pain pills left so I gave her one and walked to the bathroom. I put my clothes in the same bag as hers and took a shower.

After my shower, I climbed in the bed beside Egypt and held her tight, she had already fell asleep and I was relieved. I knew when she woke up in the morning she would have questions for me that I couldn't answer. An hour later, and I couldn't fall asleep. I laid there, holding Egypt in my arms, staring off into space. I wasn't going into the office tomorrow. I was scared that if I did go into work that she would end up leaving me because of the shit she seen me do tonight. My mind keep having flashbacks of her crying tied down to that chair. If I hadn't gotten to her in time and something worse had happened to her, I feared what I would have done.

I knew she was afraid of me now, after witnessing me kill two people. I saw the fear in her eyes while I was bathing her. I would never harm Egypt, though and I was mad at myself for not being there to stop her from getting kidnapped.

. . .

Egypt

I woke up early with Grey's arms wrapped around me. I couldn't believe all the shit that had happened in my life. I wished I'd never met Vance because all he did was bring misery and pain to my life.

The guy in the ski mask was Vance's right-hand man, Chris. Vance and Chris owed some money to the plug and the plug was threatening to kill Chris if he didn't come up with the money they owed. Chris didn't have enough money to pay the plug and Vance never told him where he put the drugs the plug fronted him.

Keisha's conniving ass had convinced Chris that Vance had run off on the plug and I knew where he was.

After they kidnapped me from work, he knocked me out with the gun in the backseat of the car. I didn't know how long I was knocked out for before he slapped me awake.

They made me get out the car at some house in the hood that looked empty. They took me to the back room and tied me up. Keisha slapped the fuck out of me and I cursed her ass out and told her when I got loose, I was beating her motherfucking ass. She laughed and Chris asked where Vance was. I didn't know where the fuck Vance was, though, so he started beating my ass.

I screamed, so they taped my mouth shut and was getting ready to ask me the same shit again when Grey and some other guy popped up to save me.

I didn't know what scared me more last night: being kidnapped and beaten or seeing Grey stab Chris and Keisha in the neck. He killed them without any hesitation.

The tattoo on his chest of the Grim Reaper with eyes like him made so much more sense now. I went from being stuck in a relationship with a psycho to falling in love with the Grim Reaper.

I wondered if the other job Grey had that he couldn't tell me about involved killing people. He had joy in his eyes when he stabbed Chris and Keisha in the neck.

The more I thought about everything, the more sense everything made. Vance didn't go missing into him and Grey got into it at the hospital and Grey asked me Vance name. After what I saw last night I don't think anybody would ever be able to find Vance again, and if they did find him I don't think he will be alive. Too much was going on in my life and I didn't have time to process it. I needed time alone to think. If Grey other job did involve killing could I be with somebody like that?

"Good morning," Grey said and I turned around to look him in his eyes. I really did love him, and he had been so good to me. How did I go from the happiest I ever been in my life to being confused and scared again.

"Be honest with me, Grey. How many people have you killed?"

He was quiet for a moment before saying, "I can't answer that."

"Is it a small number or a big number?" I asked him.

"I can't answer that," he said again. " Does your other job involve killing people and please be honest with me?" I asked him. " Egypt baby please I can't answer any of those questions. I can promise you I will never hurt you" Grey said wrapping his arms around me. I closed my eyes and shook my head because I knew my suspicions was correct. " That's a lot to process" I whispered to him. " I know" he whispered back. I cried again unsure of what was going to happen with me and Grey. He held me the whole time until I calmed down. " What do I do know" I asked Grey wiping the tears from my face. " You stay with me and trust that no matter what I do on my other job that I will always keep you protected and safe" he said. Shaking my head again I got up and went into the bathroom to handle my hygiene. After I handled my hygiene, I walked back into the room and picked up my cell-phone to call my job. My face was too fucked up to go to work.

I told them I had the flu and wouldn't be able to work this week. They didn't take the news well and told me I had missed too many days, and they think it's best that they let me go.

Grey was still laying in the bed, watching TV, when I hung up my phone. I couldn't help it; I started crying again because so much shit was happening to me at one time. " What they say" Grey asked me. " They let me go. They said I missed to many days. I wished I never meet Vance I swear to God" I told him. "I got you Egypt. Come get back in the bed with me," Grey said, and I looked at him, surprised.

"You not going into the office today?" I asked him.

"No, I'm staying home to spend the day with you," he said. I climbed back in the bed with Grey and he held me while I cried.

Grey

I woke up and Egypt's side of the bed was empty.

"Egypt !" I yelled, but I had a feeling in my gut that she had left. I knew when she asked those questions yesterday morning, she had figured out what I did on my other job.

I got out the bed and looked at my phone and saw I had a security alert. She had slipped out at 5:34 a.m. and it was now 7:26 a.m. I called her phone and she answered.

"Where are you?" I asked her.

"I need a mental break for a few weeks. I'm going away to clear my mind," she replied.

"Man, don't do this, Lil Mama. Come back home," I begged. I felt a sharp pain in my chest. "I'm not saying it's over, Grey, unless that's what you want, I just need some time alone to think," Egypt said softly .

I got quiet for a minute. I knew I could find out where she was, but would that make shit better or worse?

Man, fuck. This was why I didn't do relationships.

I guess she took my silence as me saying it was over because she hung up. I tried to call her back, but she didn't answer. I called back again, and she sent a text message.

Future: boarding plane so I am putting my phone on airplane mode. If you think it is best we end our relationship, I understand. I love you Grey. Ttyl

Me: PLANE??? GOING WHERE EGYPT? YOU LOVE ME???

I stared at my phone for about two minutes until I got mad and threw it against the wall. I heard the screen crack before it hit the floor.

I walked in the closet and all her clothes were still there. I wondered if she had taken the car, so I went downstairs, and the car was still there. Maybe she was planning on coming back to me, after all.

Egypt wasn't wrong for wanting some time to clear her mind. She has been through a lot. I was being selfish but I didn't care. We can figure this out together. We can go on a vacation together. Egypt had one week to return back home or I was going to go get her myself and bring her back.

I went in the bathroom and took a shower. I got dressed and headed out the door. I needed to go to the Apple store to get another phone.

After leaving the Apple store, I headed to my office. I called my tech guy as soon as I sat down at my desk. I gave him Egypt's name and he told me to give him a few hours and he would let me know what he found. When he hung up I tried calling Egypt again but her phone was still off. She was probably still on the plane.

I texted my brother and asked if he was going to be at his soul food restaurant around lunch time. He texted me back and told me he would. I told him I was coming through to talk to him and put my phone down on my desk.

Lunch time came and I headed toward Black's restaurant. He was sitting at a table in the back, waiting for me. I headed toward the table.

"Yo," he said to me, and I dapped him up.

" You hungry he asked" I shook my head no and sat down

"What's wrong with you?" he asked, but I didn't respond.

"Are you in love with Jordan?" I asked him a few moments later. He frowned and leaned back in his seat.

"Yea, you know I am," he replied.

"How do you know you love her?" I asked him.

"Jordan is my peace. Just hearing her voice or being around her brings me peace. We been broken up all this time and I still think about her every day," he said.

I thought about the way I felt around Egypt and how I didn't want to be with anybody else. Being with her made me happy. I realized then I was in love with Egypt.

"Do you think Jordan will ever give you another chance?" I asked him.

I knew our situations were completely different. He had cheated on Jordan a lot, and I'd killed a lot of people, but we were both in love so I was curious what his answer would be.

"When you really love somebody, you do what it takes to have them in your life. I didn't fight for Jordan in the past, but I'm not letting her get away a second time," he replied.

My phone rang, interrupting our conversation. It was my tech guy, letting me know Egypt was in Cancun, Mexico. After I hung up the phone I put it back down on the table.

" Has something happened with you and Egypt?" Black asked me.

" Shit complicated but we gone work it out" I replied.

" Are you in love with her" he asked me.

" Yes" I responded looking him in his eyes.

" Well I be damned. I never thought I would see the day. You just had to be like me and fall in love with one of the Harris sisters" Black joked.

I stayed at the restaurant with him another fifteen minutes before leaving and going back to work. I called my realtor when I made it back inside my office. I needed her to look for another building for me. After work, I went home and fixed a shot of 1942. Egypt hadn't even been gone long and I missed the fuck out of her. I didn't know what made Egypt different from the other girls I fucked, but I knew she was it for me.

I sat at my bar and took shot after shot. By the time I made it upstairs, I was so drunk, all I could do was fall in the bed and pass out.

Egypt

When we landed in Mexico I was so happy to get off the plane. Flying always made me sick. I had a three-week reservation booked at The Royal Cancun, so I caught a taxi from the airport to downtown Mercado 28 to shop and get everything I needed to be comfortable. I caught another taxi to my villa and got checked in.

When I got inside my villa I pulled out my phone and looked at the message Grey sent me. I knew he was mad I left while he was asleep, but if I waited until he was up, I probably would have never left.

I slipped out the house and walked to the entrance of Shoal Creek where my Uber was waiting for me. Leaving my car and clothes was my way of showing Grey I had plans on coming back.

The last couple of months had been full of drama and I needed a break from everybody. Plus, Grey other job was scary and dangerous. Picking up my phone I dreaded calling my sisters. " Hey" Syria answered the phone and said. " Hey, I'm adding Jordan to the call hold on" I told her. I dialed Jordan number and merged the calls when she answered. "Jordan, Syria" I said making sure the three way was working. " What" Jordan replied and Syria laughed. " So guess where I'm at?" I asked both of my sisters. " Grey house" Syria said laughing. Jordan mean ass didn't say anything. " Noooo I'm not in the US" I replied. " Yes the fuck you better be" Jordan snapped at me. " Um Egypt you playing right?" Syria asked me. " No I'm very serious. I needed a mental break so I made me reservations in Cancun and flew out" I told them. " MEXICO" they both yelled. I knew they was going to overreact. " Egypt please please tell me you didn't go to Mexico by yourself. You know they have a Cartel right and sex trafficking?" Syria asked me. "Guys people vacation in Cancun all the time I'm fine" I replied. " No smart people take GROUP trips out of the country so they don't end up dead or sold. But you obviously was dropped on your head as a child" Jordan yelled at me. " Calm down Jordan" Syria said to her. " Look guys I really needed a mental break. I promise I'm fine. I will be home in three weeks." I told them. " THREE WEEKS" they both yelled and I hung up the phone. A few seconds later my phone starting vibrating. I didn't waste my time looking because I knew it was my sisters messaging the group chat cussing me out. We did everything together so I understood why they was upset. They didn't know all the things I been through the last couple of weeks and I wanted to keep it that way

I put on a bathing suit and went outside to take a swim. When I finished, I took a shower and laid in the bed. It wasn't even a full twenty four hours yet and I missed Grey so much. This was going to be a lot harder than I thought. I got my phone out and sent him a text message.

Me: Just letting you know I made it safe. Hope you are okay.

Mine: No I'm not okay. Come back home Egypt

Me: home? I'm not even sure you still want to be with me

Mine: I told you we was never breaking up. Remember that while you on your mental break. Tell them niggas out there yo' man is crazy crazy.

Me: bye crazy love you goodnight

Mine: GN

Grey hadn't told me he loved me back, but I couldn't be mad because we hadn't been together long.

I picked up the menu they'd left in the room for me and looked over it to decide what I wanted to eat. They had chicken and waffles so I called and placed me an order in for it. I loved chicken and waffles. It only took them twenty minutes for them to cook it and bring it to me. It smelled funny but I was too hungry not to eat, so I took a bite of the chicken, anyway. Before I could swallow is I was rushing to the bathroom and throwing up. After throwing up I brushed my teeth and climbed into the bed.

The next morning, I still felt sick, so I decided to skip breakfast and go to the massage parlor they had at the villa.

I felt much better after my massage, so I caught a taxi to the downtown market to walk around and enjoy the scenery. I wanted to get my sisters souvenirs but I didn't plan on staying out long. It was hot as fuck in Cancun, and I had started sweating.

I saw these pretty African art figures and knew my sisters would love them. I headed toward the seller, fanning myself. I reached the seller and pointed at the two art figures I wanted but my vision started to blur and I saw black.

"Senorita! Senorita!" somebody shouted. I opened my eyes and was on the ground with people standing over me.

They all spoke Spanish and I could barely understand what they were trying to tell me. I looked around and noticed I was still downtown at the market.

"No hablo espanol," I told the people standing over me.

One of the ladies nodded. She got up and walked away. The people helped me stand up and the lady came back with her daughter.

"Ma'am, mi madre say you fainted," the daughter told me.

"Thank you," I told the pretty little girl and smiled.

I said bye to the people standing over me and caught a taxi back to the villa to rest. When I got back to the villa, I got in the bed, feeling drained. Maybe I should have stayed in the United States. I'd been sick ever since I got on the plane to Mexico. If I didn't know any better, I would think I was pregnant, but that couldn't be possible because I got my birth control shot faithfully.

I sat up in the bed, trying to convince myself there was no way I could be pregnant, but the thought wouldn't go away. When I got up in the morning, I was going to buy a pregnancy test to put my mind at ease.

Grey

I woke up in the bed, fully clothed, about three a.m. and got up to take a shower. I tried to fall back asleep, but I couldn't sleep last night without Egypt in the bed with me.

She sent some text messages letting me know she was okay and that she loved me. I could have told her I loved her back, but I wanted to say it to her face, and not over text messages.

Zade hit me up about a mission he needed completed today, so I got up and handled my hygiene. After this mission, I was slowing down on killing people. I wasn't ready to completely stop killing, but I wouldn't do it as much now that I had Egypt in my life.

Turning my phone off I broad another private plane . I got comfortable in my seat to take a nap until I landed. A few hours later, I had arrived at my destination. The target was a guy who was blackmailing a senator.

The senator was meeting up with the target to pay the blackmail fee, but the guy wouldn't be alive long enough to spend it.

I waited hours in the dark for the target to make it back home. The senator didn't want me to stage a scene. He wasn't worried about the target killing being connected back to him.. Finally, I heard noises coming from the front door. I pulled my ski mask down and twisted my silencer on. I lifted my gun and waited. The target came through the door, but he wasn't alone. He had a female with him. They started kissing and grabbing on each other unaware that they wasn't alone in the living room.

I shoot a bullet through her skull first because I knew she would start yelling if I killed him first. I heard him say, "What the fuck," when she fell in front of him.

He reached to turn the light on, but I sent a bullet through his skull before he could reach it. He fell on top of the dead girl. I walked up to them and sent another shot through their skulls, tucked my gun, and left.

The next morning I took another private place back home to Birmingham. When I got back home I reread the messages Egypt sent me the other day. Me and Egypt didn't talk all day yesterday. I was going to message her when I got in but the text messages between us wasn't enough. Today made four days since she had been gone.

I grabbed my phone and went to cancel the reservations I had booked at the villa I knew she was staying in. Egypt thought I was waiting the full three weeks, but my reservation was for three days away. I had planned on staying two days so we could have a mini vacation and do tourists shit together, but shit didn't always go as planned.

Egypt

I laid in the bed, looking at the three pregnancy tests in my hand. I couldn't believe I was pregnant. I got up the other day and went and bought a test, thinking there was no way it would say positive. The instructions said to pee on the stick, put the cover back on it, and wait five minutes to get your results. I followed the directions and then sat a timer for five minutes before walking back into the bathroom to check the results. When I saw it was positive, I didn't believe it, so I went and bought two more tests. They were positive too.

That was two days ago, and I was still in disbelief. I could barely keep any food down, and all I wanted to do was sleep. *How the fuck did I let this shit happen?* I knew I wasn't pregnant when I left the hospital, so the baby I was carrying was Grey's baby.

I had heard that taking medicine could affect your birth control, but I'd been on the same birth control shot since I'd started fucking at seventeen.

Grabbing my phone I checked my messages for the hundredth time. I had messaged to check on Grey the other day and he hadn't responded to me yet. I was going to wait until I went back home to tell him the news. I didn't even know if he wanted kids, but I knew I was keeping my baby. If he wanted to be there for the baby, that was cool. If he said he didn't want anything to do with the baby, that was cool too. Either way, I would make sure this baby was good.

I called my sisters on three-way and put the phone on speaker.

"Yeah?" Jordan's mean ass said with an attitude. She was still mad that I was in Mexico by myself.

"What's up?" said Syria, and I took a deep breath.

"I'm pregnant," I told them both.

Syria laughed like I was telling a joke, but Jordan was quiet. Syria stopped laughing when she noticed nobody else was laughing with her.

"You joking, Egypt?" Syria asked.

"No, I took three tests and they all came back positive," I said and started crying.

"Shut yo' crybaby ass up. You weren't crying when you was fucking," Jordan snapped.

"Stop being mean to her, Jordan. Egypt, we are surprised but happy for you," Syria said.

"Does Grey know y'all about to have a baby, Egypt? Because you are having that damn baby," Jordan asked.

I stopped crying and told her, "I am going to wait to tell him when I get home. And I didn't say I wasn't having my baby."

The call dropped before anybody else could say anything, so we started messaging in the group chat. The service in Mexico sucked ass.

I got up and got dressed after I finished talking to them. I never got their souvenirs, so I took a taxi back downtown to the market.

I wondered why Grey wasn't responding to my messages. He was probably off killing somebody somewhere, but he could have at least sent a message, letting me know he was okay. I could send him another text message, but I feel like I shouldn't have to. He should want to hear from me as much as I want to hear from him. I hated feeling like I cared more about him than he cared about me.

I spent more time at the market than I had planned on but they had so much stuff to look at.

I was exhausted by the time I made it back, so I ordered soup from room service and jumped in the shower while I waited for it to be delivered.

After my shower, I ate my soup and went to sleep. I woke up the next morning to somebody knocking on the door. I looked at my phone and it was nine in the morning. It had to be room service, but I had no idea why they were here.

"Coming!" I yelled and got out the bed to walk to the door. I opened the door and was surprised to see Grey standing in front of me. He looked so good. He was dressed in all black again, but this time, he had on a black shirt, black shorts, and black Air Jordans.

"Lil Mama," he called, and I moved out the way to let him in the villa. I left him in the room by himself while I went in the bathroom to brush my teeth and wash my face. I hid the three pregnancy tests under the sink so he wouldn't see them.

I hated to admit it, but I missed him so much and I was happy he was here. He had a black bag in his hand, so I hoped he was staying for a few days.

I walked back in the room, and he was sitting on the couch waiting for me.

Grey

I canceled my reservation at the villa last night and changed my flight to this morning. I was done waiting for Egypt to come back home so I booked t next flight to come and get her.

It only took us a couple of hours to fly to Mexico, so I made it here a little after eight in the morning. I knocked on her room door and waited until she came to the door. She opened it in little ass shorts and a tank top. Damn, I missed this girl. She didn't look mad when she was me so I'm taking that as a good sign.

She went into the bathroom, probably to handle her hygiene because I could tell I had just woken her up. I sat on the couch and waited on her to come out the bathroom.

The villa she was staying in was nice and they had a little bit of everything here for their guests.

Egypt's fine ass came out the bathroom and sat beside me on the couch.

"What are you doing here, Grey?" she asked.

"I came to spend the day with you before we go back home tomorrow," I told her. "Tomorrow? My villa is booked for three weeks," Egypt said.

"Shit happens, but we flying home tomorrow," I replied.

She shook her head and then burst out laughing. I didn't know what was funny because I was dead ass serious.

"Grey, give me one good reason why I should cut my time short here," Egypt said.

I really could have given her little ass more than one good reason, but my dick had been hard since I laid eyes on her and I was done with the conversation.

I leaned down and kissed her. Damn, I missed these lips.

We kissed as I reached under her tank top and played with her nipples. I stopped kissing her to suck on her neck. She moaned and I bit her neck. I picked her up and carried her to the bed. Taking off her tank top, I took turns sucking on both of her nipples. I kissed down her stomach and removed her shorts and panties. I placed kisses on her pussy and then kissed her clit.

"Grey, please." She moaned, but I wanted to take my time.

I put her clit in my mouth and sucked on it softly for a minute before taking my tongue and licking from the top of her pussy down to her asshole and then licking her from her asshole to her clit. I put my tongue on her clit and licked it up and down. I kept licking her clit until I felt her legs tremble. I stopped licking her clit and bit down on it. She screamed and came in my mouth. " Good girl daddy missed this good ass pussy" I told her before lowering my head back down between her legs. I licked the cum that was leaking out of her pussy. After licking all her cum up I put my tongue in her Pussy and tongue fucked her. I tongue fucked her until she started whimpering and trembling. I wanted her next but to be on my dick so I stopped what I was doing and stood up to take my clothes off. I placed her legs over my shoulders and grabbed her left foot to put her toes in my mouth. I sucked on her toes and then did the same to her right foot. I took her toes out of my mouth and grabbed her hips to lift them.

"Ahhhhh!" Egypt moaned while I slid my dick in her pussy.

"Damn." I groaned and started fucking Egypt with deep, hard strokes.

"Baby, pleaseee, it's too much!" Egypt screamed.

"It's yours. It's all yours. Take it for me like a girl " I said and increased my speed, fucking her faster. Egypt started moving her hips and fucking me back. The sight of my dick sliding in and out of her good ass pussy almost made me nut fast. I reached between her legs and rubbed on her clit. " Grey" she screamed out my name and started shaking. " Are you my good girl Egypt?" I asked her while putting her clit in between my fingers and pinching it. " Oh Fuckkkk Yess" Egypt yelled and squirted. I pulled my dick out of her and lifted her pussy to my mouth to eat all the pussy juice she'd squirted out. When I finished I flipped her on her back and she got in position. I grabbed a head full of her hair and slid in her pussy from the back, pounding her pussy hard. She screamed loud as fuck, but I kept pounding her pussy.

"Grey, please," she begged. Her pussy juice had made a big mess on the bed and I felt my nut rising.

"This my pussy, Egypt!" I moaned and nutted all in her pussy.

I fell on the bed beside Egypt and picked her up to lay her on top of me. I wrapped my arms around her tight and inhaled her scent. She wrapped her hands around my stomach and we laid wrapped up in each other's arms until we dozed off.

I woke up a couple of hours later and Egypt was still on top of me, asleep.

"Wake up, Lil Mama," I whispered in her ear and shook her gently. It took a couple of minutes to wake her, but she got up. We took a shower together and got dressed.

Egypt

I could have slept a whole week after the way Grey dicked me down. After sex, we got up and got dressed. He was excited about us going somewhere to do something he had planned.

We got a taxi and he told the cab driver to take us to some place called Xplore Theme park. We pulled up twenty minutes later and it was huge.

"Come on," Grey said, and took hold of my hand. He went to the ticket booth and told them we wanted two packages that included everything. The guy handed him the tickets and we walked inside.

The first thing I noticed was people riding boats in the prettiest blue water I had ever seen. I looked around in amazement. The theme park was surrounded by some many pretty green trees that I wonder if we was in the middle of a jungle.

"I want us to take a boat ride on the river through the caverns and then go ziplining," Grey said excitedly. I didn't ever think I'd seen him smile so big. I was happy that me and him was about to experience something together that he made him smile like that. I was so happy that it didn't register that he said ziplining until we started walking toward the boats. I stopped walking to look up at him.

"Ziplining?" I asked, to make sure I wasn't mistaken. He pointed at the sky, and I looked up. There were people going fast as fuck over a long ass, thin ass line in the sky. I watched them in horror praying they didn't fall. Grey must have really lost his goddamn mind. I wasn't getting my Black ass in the sky to zipline. I couldn't even swim, so what happens if I fall?

"Oh, hell naw I'm not doing that ," I told his ass. This nigga was crazy.

Grey kept walking like he couldn't hear, but I bet his ass would be flying on that thin ass line in the sky by his damn self.

We got to the river and put on the life jackets they handed us. Grey took the paddles and we got on the boat. The ride on the river through the cavern was relaxing and interesting. The cavern was a big cave that had rocks forming everywhere, especially hanging from the top of the cavern.

Grey paddled us through the whole thing and it was so romantic. After the boat ride, Grey took his crazy ass to the zipline and rode it across the sky all the way to the other side and all the way back. When he got off the zipline, he was happy and excited.

"Your turn," Grey said to me smiling and I turned around and walked away like he did when I told his ass the first time I wasn't ziplining. There was a sign saying kids under the age of seven and pregnant women were not allowed to ride the zipline. I couldn't get on it, anyway, because of the baby, but he didn't know that.

We got a taxi back to the villa and took another shower together. After we got out the shower, he picked up the room service menu and asked what I wanted to eat. I told him to just order a broccoli and cheddar soup. He made a face but didn't ask me why I was eating soup for dinner. I wondered how long food would make me sick. I knew Grey was going to notice something was wrong with me soon.

"Are you going back home with me tomorrow?" he asked, and I nodded yes.

I was going to tell him about the baby whenever we made it to the house tomorrow. I was worried about how he was going to take the news, but all I could do was hope for the best, but be prepared for the worst.

Grey

We woke up the next morning and got ready to head to the plane I'd booked. Yesterday was my first time at Xplore and I planned on bringing Egypt back in the future so we could go there again.

I thought Lil Mama was going to get on the zip line, but she wasn't fucking with it.

We made it back home before lunch time, so I took Egypt to my brother's restaurant to eat. She didn't want breakfast because flying made her sick. The server led us to our seat and we both ordered sweet tea to drink.

"You sure you okay? You still look sick, Lil Mama," I asked Egypt.

"Yeah, it takes my stomach a few hours to settle after a flight. I'm about to run to the ladies' room. I will be right back," Egypt said, getting up from the table. I picked up the menu, trying to decide whether I wanted BBQ or fried chicken. "Hey, baby, I been calling you," I heard a woman say. I looked up and Nene was standing at my table, smiling. *Did this crazy bitch just call me baby?*

"Man, get the fuck on," I told Nene, but she didn't move.

"Baby, I miss you so much," this crazy ass girl said like she hadn't heard me tell her to get the fuck on.

"Who yo' baby?" Egypt asked Nene, walking back up to the table.

"Who the fuck are you?" Nene turned to Egypt and asked.

"My woman," I answered before Egypt could say anything.

"Your woman? But you was just fucking on me not too long ago, Grey!" Nene's ass screamed.

"Girl, he just told you who I was, so keep that shit moving," Egypt said, laughing at Nene behaving like a crazy woman in front of all these people.

"You laughing, but I hope you ready to be a stepmother," Nene said to Egypt. Now I was laughing because I knew this crazy bitch was lying.

"Awww, how sweet. I'm pregnant too. I'm sure my baby would love having a brother or sister so close in age," Egypt replied to Nene. I stopped laughing because I didn't know shit about any babies, but now, all of a sudden, I was supposed to have two on the way.

Nene turned red in the face and tried to push Egypt, but Egypt punched the girl in the nose.

"She hit me!" Nene screamed, holding her nose. She tried to hit Egypt back but I pushed her ass and she fell. I put Egypt behind my back and stood in front of her. " Bitch he won't always be there to protect you" Nene yelled standing back up.

" Girl he protecting you. You lucky I'm pregnant or I would have really whooped yo ass" Egypt responded.

Black ran from his office in the back to see what all the commotion was about. He saw me standing in front of Egypt and told Nene she had to leave. She tried fussing with him but black wasn't hearing it. Black grabbed Nene and escorted her out the restaurant and Egypt sat back down at the table and picked up the menu like nothing had happened. Black came back in the restaurant and walked back to the table we were sitting at. I sat down shocked at what the fuck just happened.

"Bro, what happened?" he asked, but I stared at Egypt, wondering if she had lost her damn mind.

She looked up at me and rolled her eyes. "One of your brother's hoes don't have no house training, so she caused a scene about Grey getting her pregnant. I told her ass welcome to the club, and she didn't like that, so she pushed me and I popped her in the nose," Egypt told Black. He looked at me like I was the crazy one.

"You got two babies on the way?" he asked.

"Man, hell naw," I told his ass. He burst out laughing.

"You got one baby on the way?" he asked, and hell, I looked at Egypt's ass again.

She looked at both of us and rolled her eyes again. "Yes, he do," she said to Black.

Black looked at the expression on my face and fell out laughing even harder.

Egypt

Grey and that crazy bitch who had just been escorted out had me fucked up.

I looked at the menu and didn't even want to eat anything anymore. I put the menu back on the table, grabbed my purse, and stood up.

"Egypt , what you are doing?" Grey asked, but I didn't waste my time responding. I walked out the restaurant. When I got outside, I went and stood by his car and waited.

He had three minutes to bring his ass out that restaurant or I was calling an Uber to come get me.

He came out the restaurant a few seconds later, unlocked the car, and I opened the door and got in.

"Ay, I don't care about your attitude. Yo' lil ass better not open another car door in front of me," he snapped, getting in the car.

I closed my eyes and leaned back against the seat. I planned on telling Grey I was pregnant after we left the restaurant and made it home, but his little hoe messed my plan up.

The rest of the ride home was quiet. When we pulled up at the house, I wanted to be petty and open the door again, but I knew by his tone, when he snapped, he was dead ass serious about not opening another car door in front of him.

When I got in the house, I went in the kitchen to cut some fruit up to eat while he brought our bags in.

Grey came downstairs and went to the bar and fixed him a shot of 1942. I got up to wash my bowl out and headed up the stairs. He followed me out the kitchen and into the bedroom.

I began unpacking and put everything where it belonged while Grey sat on the bed, watching me.

At the bottom of my bag were the three pregnancy tests I had taken. I picked them up and handed them to him. He stared at the test for a minute before handing them back to me.

"When did you find out?" he asked.

"The day I sent you a text message and you didn't respond," I told him.

"Don't you think you should have told me as soon as you found out?" he asked.

"I wanted to tell you tonight when we got home, but your lil hoe messed up my plans," I said with an attitude.

"I cut that girl off before I even met you," he said.

"Tell me the truth, did you know about her baby?" I asked him.

"Lil Mama, that bitch lying. I have never fucked that girl raw, and I always check my condoms after I fuck. If she is pregnant, it ain't mine," he said all nonchalantly like he had no worries in the world.

"She said she been calling you. Y'all was talking behind my back? You cheating on me?" I walked up in his face and asked. I told his ass what would happen if he cheated on me, and I meant what I said. "Man, the last couple of weeks, I have been getting private calls, but they never say anything when I answer. It had to be her playing on my phone. I would have never got in a relationship if I wanted to still fuck off," he told me. He got up and wrapped his arms around me to hold me.

He never said how he felt about me being pregnant and I didn't know if I believed him or not about that girl's baby not being his. If she was pregnant and it was his, I didn't even know if I had the right to be mad about it because he fucked her before I came in the picture. I knew the truth would come to light about the situation though so I let it go.

He kissed me on the forehead, and I walked out of his arms to get in the shower. In the shower, I leaned my head against the shower wall and let the hot water ease my stress. Why was being in love so difficult?

Tomorrow, I would make a doctor's appointment to check on the baby and then start job hunting. No matter what, I would make sure this baby was okay and well taken care of.

I got my body wash and poured it on my African body net.

"Let me do it," Grey said, startling me. Grey got in the shower with me and took my African body net out my hand. He cleaned every inch of my body and I cleaned every inch of his.

"Are you mad about the baby?" I asked him.

"Naw, I'm not mad, just surprised. I'ma always be there for you and the baby, though. That's something you don't ever have to worry about," he told me.

I pulled his head down to me and kissed him. He picked me up and carried me to the bed where we had makeup sex and went to sleep.

Egypt

Morning sickness kicked my ass this morning, but I was determined to get out and enjoy my day. My doctor's appointment was in a couple of days, and I couldn't wait to have my first ultrasound.

Last night, after Grey said he was going to be there for me and my baby, I told him I accepted everything that came with him. I was honest with him and told him seeing that side of him scared me, but I really did love him. I saw the relief in his face when I told him that. He was worried I was still thinking about leaving him, especially after that drama yesterday with that crazy ass girl in the restaurant. We had to get better at communicating with each other because I planned on being in Grey's life for a very long time. Tonight, he was taking me out on a date, and I wondered where he was taking me. He wouldn't tell me since he wanted it to be a surprise.

I was heading to meet with my sisters so we could have a girls' day of pampering. They decided to stay at Black's house until they found a house here because I wasn't moving back to Tuscaloosa and they didn't want us to be separated.

I pulled up at the hair salon and got out. My sisters had texted me five minutes ago and told me they had already made it.

When I walked inside, they were sitting in the waiting

area. I walked over to give them a hug. We still had ten minutes until it was our appointment time, so I took a seat beside them.

"So, I heard you showed your ass yesterday," Syria said and burst out laughing.

"Tell Black to stop being messy," I said and started laughing with her.

"Hmmm… Well, Black says his brother don't lie, and if Grey said that ain't his baby, then that ain't his baby," said Jordan. I stared at her, shocked. I couldn't believe her mean ass was listening to Black or taking up for Grey. "You and Black fucking?" I asked Jordan and started laughing even harder.

"Girl, no, we just decided to be friends," Jordan said. I didn't believe her, but I changed the subject.

"My doctor's appointment is a couple of days away and I am so nervous," I admitted to them.

"Can I come?" asked Syria.

"Not this time. Grey is coming with me, but when I find out what I'm having, I want both of you there with us," I told them.

One of the hair stylists approached us and told us they were ready for us. I loved coming to this hair salon because they didn't play about staying on schedule.

I decided to get my hair flat ironed and wear it with a middle part.

After we finished getting our hair done, they got in my Range Rover and we headed toward the mall.

"Do you know what the dress code is for your date tonight?" Syria asked as I pulled in the mall's parking lot.

"He told me the dress code is formal, but I already know what I am wearing. That's not what I am here to get," I told them as we walked in the mall.

"What are we here for then?" Jordan asked, but I didn't

respond. I walked for about three minutes until I saw the store I wanted to go in and headed that way. "Girl, I know you did not drag us to the mall to go to a sex store," Jordan said, and I laughed.

"Come on," I told them and walked inside.

"Is there anything I can help y'all with?" a lady walked up to us and asked.

"Yes, where are your vibrating panties?" I asked her.

"Right this way," she said and led me to where they were.

"That's why yo' ass pregnant now, being fast in the ass," Syria said, shaking her head.

I purchased the panties and we left the mall to get our nails and toes done. By the time I made it home, I had two hours to take a shower, do my makeup, and get dressed.

Grey

My mind had been on Egypt being pregnant all day. I was ready for her doctor's appointment, so I knew everything was okay with my baby. Lil Mama had been texting me all day, asking for clues on where I was taking her tonight, but I wouldn't tell her.

I left work and headed home so I could get showered and dressed. When I walked through the door, I heard music, so I knew Egypt was still getting dressed. I headed upstairs and she was in the mirror, doing her makeup.

"Hey, Lil Mama," I said and kissed her on her forehead. I headed to the bathroom to take a shower so I could get dressed. When I got out the shower, Egypt was dressed in a long, blue dress with a thigh slit. She looked amazing.

I walked in my closet and put on black pants and a blue shirt to match Egypt. Fifteen minutes later, we walked out of the house. I opened the door for Egypt and helped her get in the car. When I got in the driver's seat, Egypt handed me a small black remote controller.

"What is this?" I asked her.

"I have on vibrating panties, and that is the control to them." I looked at her, speechless for a second. She smiled, and I pressed the button.

"Oh!" Egypt gasped, and my dick got hard. I pressed the button again and she reached out to grab my hand to squeeze it. I let it continue for about fifteen seconds before pressing the button down and holding it to cut it off. My Lil Mama wanted to be freaky tonight and I was with the shits.

I put the controller in my pocket and headed to Perry Steakhouse. I had to call in a favor to get us reservations because it was booked for the night.

When we got to the restaurant, I got out to open the door for Egypt and led her inside. The host greeted us and asked for our name. I told her and she led us to our table.

Perry Steakhouse was the most expensive restaurant in Birmingham, but it was worth every penny.

I waited until the server approached us and asked our drink order before turning on the controller. Egypt could barely say sweet tea. I hit it a couple more times to increase the speed and she reached out to grab the tablecloth and bit her lip. Egypt's sex faces were so fucking beautiful. The server walked away, and I cut it off.

"I can't wait until we get home so I can torture you," she said and I chuckled.

"I'm with whatever," I replied. All throughout dinner, I would cut the vibrator on and wait until I knew she was close to nutting and cut it off.

"I'm going to the bathroom to take off my panties. They are soaked," she whispered and stood up to walk away. My dick was so hard, I was afraid to stand. I took deep breaths to calm down and prayed Egypt didn't want dessert.

Fuck this shit, I was ready to go home. I signaled the waitress for the check. When Egypt came out the bathroom, I stood and took hold of her hand.

"Come on, Lil Mama," I said, and we walked out the restaurant, holding hands. I opened the car door for her and helped her in. I got inside the car and pulled off.

Egypt started rubbing her hands up and down my dick and then unzipped my pants.

"Man, chill, Egypt," I told her ass, but she didn't listen. She pulled my dick out my briefs and licked the tip of it. I prayed we made it home safe without crashing. She spat on my dick and then began sucking on it. She gagged a few times before deep throating me.

"Fuck!" I groaned. She kissed the tip of my dick, then moved her mouth away and sat back. I laughed and put my dick back in my pants. I didn't want to hear shit when we made it in this house.

Ten minutes later, we pulled up at the house and I jumped out and opened the door for Egypt. "Bring that ass." I told her

She laughed and I took her hand and rushed inside. As soon as the security alarm was set, I picked Lil Mama up and took her ass to the kitchen. I pulled her dress up and was greeted with her pretty ass pussy. I sucked on her clit until she was shaking. " Are you ready to fill my mouth with that good ass pussy juice" I asked Egypt" " Damn" she moaned and nutted in my mouth. I flipped her little ass over and pulled my dick out my pants, sliding my dick inside her pussy and hitting her with a few long strokes. I wrapped my hands in her hair and pulled her head back, increasing my speed and pounding her pussy.

"Grey, slow down," she moaned, but I didn't want to hear that shit.

"No, be my good girl and take this dick." I continued to

pound her pussy as she screamed my name over and over. I spread her ass cheeks and spit on her ass whole. I slid my thumb in her ass. " Grey I'm finna nut" she moaned throwing her ass back. I smacked her on the ass and she came all over my dick. I wonder how the fuck did her pussy get so wet and tight at the same time. " Good girl" I said and pulled out of her.

I placed a kiss on her pussy before I started eating her from the back. I moved up further and put my tongue in her ass. I put my hand in between her legs and rubbed her clit while I tongue fucked her ass until she came again in my mouth. .

"This my pussy, Egypt?" I asked her and she moaned yes. I put my dick back inside of her, and fucked her hard. I was pounding her pussy so hard she couldn't do anything but take it. . "Say this your pussy, Grey," I told her and moaned. Damn, this pussy good as fuck.

"This... This... This your pussy, Grey!" she yelled and I felt my nut rising. I slow stroked her pussy until I felt her pussy muscles tightening up around my dick again. " My good girl ready to cum with daddy" I asked her increasing my strokes. She moaned and started trembling. " Damn I love this pussy" I groaned. A few seconds later we both was cumming at the same time.

I picked her up and carried her upstairs. Laying her down on her bed, I was ready to start round two. I sucked and fucked Egypt all night.

Egypt

The next couple of days passed by and me and Grey were doing great. Today was my first doctor's appointment and I was nervous. After I signed a stack of papers asking a million medical questions, they told us to have a seat in the first waiting room.

Grey had driven me here. I told him he didn't have to come if he didn't want to, but he said he wanted to. It took almost fifteen minutes before I heard my name called. I went inside a dark room with a big exam table in the middle of it. The lady inside handed me a sheet and told me to go to the bathroom to strip from the waist down. I went in the bathroom and took off my pants and panties. When I came back out, she had me lay down on the examination table. She put gel on a long, white tube and put it inside of me. I looked at the screen and there was a small dot in my stomach. I couldn't believe I was about to be somebody's mother.

I looked over at Grey and he stared at the screen, smiling. I loved when he smiled because it didn't happen a lot. The lady took the tube out of me and cleaned it off. She went to her computer and printed off a picture of my ultrasound. I was six weeks and three days pregnant. She said my next ultrasound wouldn't be until I was sixteen weeks. At sixteen weeks, we would be able to hear the baby's heartbeat and learn the baby's sex. We went back out to the waiting room to wait on my doctor to call us back. Grey held my hand while we waited.

Ten minutes later, my doctor called my name. The doctor led us to a room and handed me a gown to put on. I took off my clothes and handed them to Grey and put on the gown the doctor had given me.

She came back in the room a few minutes later and did a quick exam of my body and told me everything appeared fine. She told me I should try not to stress too much, especially during my first trimester. She asked if we had any questions and Grey asked if it was normal that I got so sick, I wouldn't eat. She told him it was normal, but that she would prescribe some medicine to help with nausea and prenatal vitamins. She gave me a pamphlet full of pregnancy questions and answers and scheduled an appointment to come back in four weeks.

Grey

Me and Egypt left the doctor's office, holding hands. I couldn't believe I was about to be a father. I opened the door for Egypt and helped her get in the car. I got in the passenger side and headed toward CVS.

"Thank you for going with me," Egypt said.

I smiled at her and asked, "Can I have the ultrasound picture?" She smiled and handed it to me. I stuck it in front of me on my dashboard.

When we pulled up at CVS, I told her to stay in the car and I would run in to get her medicine. I came back out ten minutes later with everything I needed. I got back in and headed toward Nene's house.

"Where are we going?" Egypt asked.

"To put an end to this," I told her.

"End to what, Grey?" she asked, but I didn't respond. I saw Nene's car in her driveway and was happy she was here. I pulled up behind Nene's car and got the pregnancy test I bought out of CVS. I got out and went to open the door for Egypt. "Who lives here, Grey?"

"Nene," I told her, and she stopped walking.

"Come on, Lil Mama, this ends today," I told her and grabbed her hand. I walked up to Nene's door and rang the bell. Nene came to the door a couple of minutes later and asked who it was. Egypt and I were both quiet until she opened the door.

"Why the fuck you bring her to my house, Grey?" Nene screamed.

"Go take this." I ignored her question and handed her the pregnancy test. She threw the test on the floor.

"I'm not taking shit. I will see you in court," she said and tried to close the door. I put my foot in the door to stop her from closing it, then pulled my gun out and pointed it at her.

"Man, I don't got time for this shit. Go take this fucking test, now." I heard Egypt gasp, but I didn't give a fuck. I was over the bullshit ass games.

"Fine, I lied. Are you happy?" she screamed and tried to push the door closed.

"Look, Shawty, I'm losing my patience. Go take the test and we all gon' sit in the living room and wait on the results together."

Nene started crying but she picked up the test and went in the bathroom to take it. Me and Egypt had a seat in the living room. I could tell Egypt felt uncomfortable, but the doctor said stress was bad for the baby, so it was time to handle this situation.

She came back out and I put a timer on my phone for five minutes. Nobody said anything until the timer beeped.

"Go," I told Nene and she jumped up and ran to the bathroom to get the test. She brought it back out and showed me the results. I knew this crazy ass bitch was lying.

"Don't ever contact me again," I said, grabbing my girl's hand and walking back outside to the car. Nene slammed her front door as soon as we walked out of it. I helped Lil Mama get in the car, then I got in and pulled off.

"I have one more place to take you. Do you want to eat before we go there or after?" I asked Egypt.

"I don't have a big appetite so we can just grab something after," Egypt said.

I nodded and drove downtown. I pulled up in front of a building not too far away from my security firm. I got out the car and went to open the door for Egypt. She followed me to the door of the office, and I took the keys out of my pocket to unlock them.

"I thought you were opening your next security firm in Florida? What will this building be for?" Egypt asked.

"Hell, whatever you want this building for. You can open your own counseling office for kids or do whatever you want with it," I told Egypt and handed her the keys.

"Grey, what the fuck? Is this really my office? Stop playing," Egypt said, looking at me. "This yours, Lil Mama," I told her.

"When did you do this, Grey?" Egypt asked shocked.

"I had my realtor start looking while you was in Cancun. I want us to walk through it together to make sure you like it, then we have to go to my realtor's office so you can sign the papers." Egypt wrapped her arms around me and started crying. I wasn't expecting her to cry. I figured she would kiss me or some shit. I wondered if the pregnancy had anything to do with it. I made a mental note to buy a pregnancy book so I could know what to expect.

"Are you okay, Egypt? I thought you would be happy," I asked, wiping the tears from her face.

"I am so happy. I love you so much," she said.

"I love you, too, Lil Mama. We locked in for life, now stop crying and come check out your new building," I told her and grabbed her hand.

" Do you really love me" she asked while we walked through the office space.

" Yes I am in love with you. You are it for me Egypt. I plan on making you my wife" I replied. She stopped walking and reached for my face to kiss me. I meet her half way. She was back crying so I wiped the tears off her face when we finished kissing.

After we walked through her new office, she FaceTimed her sisters and shared the news with them. They were happy like I had gotten it for all of them and I liked that. I hoped Black got his shit together and fixed things with Jordan.

We left and I took her to sign the papers at my realtor's office and get some food. Egypt accepted me for who I am. She loved me regardless of the fact that I got a rush from killing people. She will spend the rest of her life getting treated like a queen because she fell in love with a boss flaws and all.

EPILOGUE

Egypt

I didn't see how people stayed pregnant for more than forty weeks. I hit forty weeks today and I planned on demanding the doctor induce me at my appointment because I couldn't do this shit anymore. My feet were so swollen, it hurt to walk. My back hurt because this baby I was carrying had me big as a house. I couldn't find a comfortable position to sleep in to save my damn life. I always had to pee and was emotional as fuck. My husband was aggravating as fuck, asking how I felt every ten minutes. I was over it and this baby had to get its walking papers today.

I looked down at my rose gold fourteen carat wedding ring and smiled. I thought back to the day of my gender reveal.

At first, I didn't want to have a gender reveal, but my sisters and everybody who worked at my counseling office kept asking me to have one. I gave in and let my sisters throw me one. The theme was Ghost or Ghoul, and everything was decorated so beautifully.

If people thought I was having a boy, they had on blue

ghost shirts. If people thought I was having a girl, they had on pink ghoul shirts. Me and Grey wore blue ghost shirts.

When it was time to find out the gender, my sisters blind-folded me and Grey and told me to count to ten then take the blindfold off. I did as asked, and when I lifted my blindfold, Grey was down on one knee, in front of me, asking me to marry him. Of course, I said yes. After he slid my ring on, my sisters brought out a congratulations cake that we had to cut to see the color of the icing inside. We cut the cake together and the icing was pink. I found out I was carrying this big headed little girl in my stomach.

Later that night, Grey asked what kind of wedding I wanted and I told him I didn't want a wedding; I was fine getting married at the courthouse. The only people I wanted there for me were my sisters because I knew they loved me, without any doubt.

A few days later, Grey told me to get up and get dressed so we could get some breakfast. Instead of going to a restaurant, we pulled up to a private jet he had booked. I boarded the plane and my sisters, Black, and Zade were already on there. He flew us all out to Vegas, and we got married.

That was four months ago and I loved every day of being married to Grey. He still worked his other job, but he had only done it a few times since we'd gotten married.

He always told me he had business out of town before he left instead of just disappearing with no communication like he did before. I still stayed up worried about his safety all night when he was gone, but I accepted all of him, even the Grim Reaper side that liked to kill people.

"Lil Mama, we have to go," my husband said. I hadn't even heard him come out of the bathroom. I stood up and followed him down the stairs, and out of our house.

We made it to the doctor's office twenty minutes later. The doctor wanted me to get another ultrasound so she could see how much this baby weighed. We did the ultrasound first, and the baby kicked me in the ribs the whole time.

After the ultrasound, we sat back down and waited for the doctor to call us back. The doctor called my name and we followed her to her room. She gave me some privacy to undress, then came back in the room.

"Hey, Mrs. Williams, how are we feeling today?" she asked.

"We're feeling like I want to be induced to get this baby out of me today," I told her ass. She laughed.

"The baby is measuring almost ten pounds, so being induced will probably be the best route," she said. I turned around to look at Grey and rolled my eyes at his ass because it was his fault I had to push out this big head ass baby. He chuckled like my attitude didn't faze him .

"Lay back and let me see if you have dilated anymore," she said. I'd been stuck at two centimeters for weeks.

She stuck her hand inside of me and I pissed on her. I didn't mean to, I just felt a rush of warm liquid rush out of me.

"Oh my, it is baby time. Your water just broke, and you are already dilated four centimeters," she said and went to grab her nurse. As soon as she walked out, I felt a sharp pain in my stomach and back. I grabbed my stomach and took deep breaths.

"Lil Mama, what's happening?" he said.

"Ah, fuck! Contraction!" I told his ass. The contraction eased up and the doctor and nurse came in the room to tell me to get in the wheelchair so they could take me to labor and delivery. A few minutes later, another contraction hit and it was worse than the first. I didn't think I could do this. It hurt too bad.

My birthing plan was to go natural, without any epidural or pain medicine, but I was about to say fuck that shit. Six hours of yelling, screaming, and crying, the doctor finally said I was at ten centimeters, and I could start pushing. It took almost twenty minutes of pushing to get this big headed ass baby out of me. I was so exhausted, I wanted to close my eyes when I finally heard her cry.

The nurse laid her on me so we could do skin to skin, then handed her to Grey so he could do skin to skin.

Lavender Sinai Williams came out nine pounds four ounces and twenty-two inches long. She looked just like me, but she had one blue eye and one brown eye like her father. I looked at my husband and smiled.

A year ago, I was stuck in a relationship with a psycho, and now I was in love with a Grim Reaper and I wouldn't have it any other way.

An hour later, Jordan, Syria, Black, and, Zade had all made it to the hospital to see Baby Lavender. They argued over who would hold her first. Grey didn't want to let anybody hold Baby Lavender at all but they weren't having it. I thought Jordan and Zade were about to jump on Grey and take Baby Lavender. Grey had made Zade Lavender's godfather and I sent a silent prayer up for any guy she dated in the future.

The End

WANT TO BE A PART OF GRAND PENZ PUBLICATIONS?

To submit your manuscript to Grand Penz Publications, please send the first three chapters and synopsis to info@grandpenz.com

Made in the USA
Monee, IL
23 May 2023

34383028R00077